The Reunion
A second chance romance

by

Stephanie Brother

Book cover designed by RomanceCoverDesigns.com

Chapter One
Muriel Tennyson

Why should I be one bit worried about seeing my old classmates at the wedding? No reason at all.

Former classmates included Cam and Hugh who were once my best friends, as well as being two of the hottest guys to walk the face of the earth. I'd thought about them often, even after I'd moved to live on the other side of the country.

But I'd blocked the guys on social media and lost all contact with them.

The prospect of seeing them again didn't worry me, because I clung to the optimistic certainty that they wouldn't be among the wedding guests. Would they?

Nevertheless, I wanted to appear my best if not stunning. Just in case.

"Okay, one of you, please tell me you brought an umbrella," I said hopefully when our cab pulled up outside the adorable Lakeview Resort.

When you've got frizzy hair, the slightest hint of water vapor in the air tends to send you into a self-centered panic, even when it's another woman's big day.

"Put your jacket over your head; it'll be fine," Poppy replied, confidently stepping out of the car with a silk scarf wrapped around her head like a Hollywood Silver Screen actress.

"We can't all be models with perfect hair," I called after her as she shut the door and sauntered toward the hotel.

The long, azalea-lined path to the entrance would have been much more appealing in the sunshine. Instead, dark gray clouds hung low overhead, and huge raindrops pelted the ground.

Even though my first thought was my hair, I did have more sympathy for Chrissy than myself. The rain fell over her wedding day, after all, and no one wants to begin married life under a storm.

"Yeah, well," Jasmine huffed, digging a jacket out of her carry-on. "If you'd let me rent a limo at the airport like I suggested, the driver would've had umbrellas for us to use. So this is kind of your fault, really."

I shook my head at my other best friend. "Oh yes, that would have been a great way to make an entry—showing up at someone else's wedding in a limo like three brash snobs from out of town."

"I'm just saying, if you come face to face with Cameron tonight with hair like a piece of cotton candy, your gal Jas isn't to blame." Jasmine shrugged.

The idea of caring about Cameron's thoughts on my appearance made me snort with derision, but Jas didn't appear convinced by my couldn't-care-less attitude. "Not that it matters; Cameron won't be here, anyway. He and Chrissy barely hung out at school."

"Oh, didn't you hear?" Jas replied casually, but with a wicked glint in her eye. "The groom is Cameron's partner on the force, so he's definitely coming. He's probably the best man." Jasmine giggled and leaped out of the car.

I stuttered a thank you to the cab driver before getting out and running to the hotel as fast as my heels would carry me, with my denim jacket tied tight around my head.

The smell of blooming flowers in the rain hit my senses like a nostalgia bomb. In my mind's eye I was back at school, running across the grounds to meet Cameron and Hugh in the library. Not that any of us were particularly big readers; we just liked the quiet in there. We'd huddle in a corner and talk about how great it would be when we escaped Georgia and make something of our lives.

That was six years ago now, and I got away but the boys stayed, nevertheless, sometimes I wonder why I'd ever expected LA to be any better than Covington.

It rains less, the whining voice in my head reminded me as I pulled open the door of the beautiful colonial-style hotel.

While Jasmine and Poppy checked in, I took a seat and kept an eye out for anyone I recognized from school. This wedding basically acted as a reunion, and I'd been looking forward to catching up with people I hadn't seen since graduation.

I hadn't expected Cameron or Hugh to be invited, though; they moved in totally different circles to Chrissy.

I'd left a sexy little floral dress hanging in my closet and cursed myself, then cursed myself again for caring. Those guys were nothing more than friends from long ago, that's all.

Friends who I never said goodbye to before leaving for college.

Friends whose calls I'd ignored a dozen times before they gave up trying to contact me.

Friends I'd blocked on social media because I could not bear to see them with other girls.

Just totally regular friends who were boys but not my boyfriends.

"Muriel, you're up," Poppy called across the lobby. "We're headed to the bar; see you in there."

I walked over to check-in where the receptionist beamed at me as I arrived at the desk, a genuine smile that I had to reflect back at her.

"Welcome to Lakeview Resort. My name's Sandy." She leaned forward and spoke in an exaggerated whisper, "Shall I book you in for a blow-dry at our spa this afternoon?"

I laughed and gratefully accepted. Evidently, denim doesn't do much to protect you from the rain.

While Sandy tapped away at her keyboard, I raked my fingers through my wet hair, but she looked up and shook her head.

"The more you touch it, the frizzier it'll get—believe me." I eyed her immaculate updo, wondering what she could possibly understand about the frizzy-hair life, and she obviously sensed my skepticism. "Bruno is a miracle worker. I wouldn't go to anyone else, and I've got you booked in with him at three. Until then, here's the key to your bungalow. Let me give you directions."

She went on to explain how to get there as it was quite some distance from the main hotel and we discussed my rental car that was being delivered later that day. Sandy would arrange to have it parked alongside the bungalow, ready for me.

"Thank you so much." I took the keys and an embossed appointment card and followed the signs to the bar, feeling happier than ever to be back in my hometown.

To get great service like that in LA, people had to know you or at least recognise you. I was starting to be recognized in places thanks to my Instagram, but it made me slightly uncomfortable, like I was only treated well because I was a '*somebody.*'

Jas was the total opposite; she'd soak up every freebie and perk available. As a talented designer and amazing friend, she deserved all the best, in my opinion; otherwise, I'd probably hate her guts.

I spotted my friends in a booth in the sleek, modern bar and headed over to join them.

"Hey there. Can I get you anything?" a server appeared at the table the moment I sat down.

"A sweet tea—" I began to reply, and Poppy narrowed her eyes at me.

"You're not drinking? This is a celebration."

"...with peach schnapps and vodka, thanks." The server and Poppy both looked satisfied, and I settled back into the booth.

Our drinks arrived quickly, and I fought my instinct to grab my phone and start taking cute photos of us all for social media. But I wanted to have a true vacation for a few days; this weekend, I wasn't a social media influencer, I was simply Muriel Tennyson, and it would be great.

And more importantly, nobody needed to see me in my current state; my hair started to dry and inevitably grow bigger by the second.

"Oh, look, there's Chrissy." Jas waved at someone over my shoulder.

I turned to see our old school friend walking toward us, already looking every inch the glowing bride in a cute white tea dress with white Converse.

I took a long sip of my spiked tea and tried to imagine what it would be like to vow fidelity to one man for the rest of your life.

The small-town girl in me yearned for exactly what Chrissy had, but a bigger part of me remained convinced I'd never be satisfied by conventional so-called domestic bliss.

"Hey y'all," Chrissy said as she arrived at our table with a smile so wide she must have had no nerves and no doubts about marriage at all. "I'm so glad all y'all could make it. How was the flight?" She slipped into our booth beside me.

"A bit bumpy," Jas replied. "The turbulence when we landed had Poppy screaming like a banshee."

"Oh, please," Poppy gave Jas a playful shove. "You practically sat in the lap of the guy next to you."

"Did you see him? He was hot." Jas's eyes widened, and she licked her lips. "And that was the only reason for our closeness, honestly."

Chrissy chuckled. "Well, I hope that's the biggest drama we have this weekend. The Weather Channel has just announced there's a series of storms and tornadoes on their way here and due to hit tomorrow, but what do they know?"

"Well, I think they know about the weather," Poppy said, and Jas took a turn to elbow her in the ribs. "Er, but I'm sure it'll be fine. Hurricanes change course all the time, don't they?"

I leaned back and mouthed 'nice save' out of view of the bride-to-be.

"Exactly." Chrissy pointed a determined finger at Poppy. "Right, I have a million things to do, so you girls enjoy yourselves, and I'll see you tonight." With that, she stood up and dashed out of the bar, glass of Champagne in hand.

"Lucky girl," Poppy said, looking wistfully at our friend's departing figure.

"Oh, please," I replied. "You ghosted a guy last month for suggesting he leave a toothbrush at your place. Now you're ready for a lifetime commitment?"

"No. I mean the party, and the dress and everything. Seems fun, that's all."

I laughed at my friend; the three of us were so different in many ways but so alike in this. "Think of it this way, we get to enjoy the party and admire the dress without having to promise to love, honor, or obey anyone at all."

"Cheers to that." Jas raised her glass, and we all joined in.

"Well, well, well, if it isn't Muri." My arm froze in the air as a familiar voice rang out beside me. Even after all this time I'd recognize that voice anywhere; it sent me hot and cold all at once. I slowly turned my head and looked up at Cameron, who stared down at me with a mischievous grin on his face.

"Shit—I mean, hi." I slammed my drink down so hard it splashed out of the glass. "Er, how are you?"

"I'm good, really good, actually. It's great to see you; it's been, what, five years?"

I needed to answer him, but I was distracted by his—um... well, everything about him.

With his lightly slicked back blond hair and his sharp cheekbones, he'd somehow matured into an even sexier guy since the last time I'd seen him, which didn't seem possible.

A smattering of freckles across his nose made him appear cute and boyish, but the body that filled out his casual sweatshirt and jeans was manly all right.

"Yes, Cameron, five years."

I recalled the last time we hung out — Cameron, Hugh, and I — and the amazing night we very nearly had. Up until then, we'd been best buddies. They'd been like brothers to me. Everything changed.

The sound of Jasmine talking very slowly and loudly, plus the pain of her kicking me under the table snapped me out of my reverie.

"Yeah, a long time," I said pointlessly, and I remembered what a state I must look after getting caught in the rain. I started trying to pat my hair down until I noticed Cameron struggling to contain his laughter.

"You don't need to do that," he said as I began to blush. "I like the 'Monica Geller in Barbados' look. It suits you."

I tried to come up with a biting retort, but all that came to mind was, *And the sexy, boy-next-door look suits you.* So I opted for a sarcastic, "Ha, ha."

"Well, I'll have to leave you ladies; Hugh and I have a round of virtual golf lined up this afternoon. We'll catch up properly at the dinner tonight, though, right?"

"Yeah, sure," Poppy said, and I gave a weak wave as he walked away.

His ass looked great in his jeans, and my thoughts briefly drifted again until Jas's fingers clicked in front of my face.

"Right," she said, folding her arms like she meant business. "What happened with you two? You've never told us anything, and we're your best friends."

"And you know everything about us," Poppy joined in, leaving me cornered.

I sucked down the last of my cocktail and shrugged. "Nothing happened. We were friends, but we haven't seen each other for a while, that's all."

"Bullshit," Poppy said. "You basically melted into a puddle at the sight of him, and he is *clearly* besotted with you. You must have at least dated."

"I'm not so sure," Jas said, stroking her chin like a TV detective. "Cameron's so happy; he's like a Labrador puppy. I don't think our Muriel would put up with that for long—that's why she always had Hugh hanging around too; he was all moody and serious."

I managed to maintain a poker face, but actually Jasmine's deduction skills impressed me. As handsome and lovely as Cameron was, his infectious optimism did sometimes too much—and so Hugh was the perfect counterbalance. It didn't hurt that they were best friends, great guys, and as cute as a couple of catalog models.

Hugh was a kind and generous guy, but he had a world-weariness that perfectly balanced Cameron's sunshine-and-rainbows attitude, even back in high school. And I was the fiery character who would keep them both in check. It would have been a great dynamic for a lifelong friendship if only things had been different.

"That's a great theory, but it's simply not true," I said. "And on a completely unrelated matter, how many dresses have you brought with you, Jas?"

She shrugged. "I dunno really, maybe six?" Jasmine could win Olympic gold at over packing.

"Cool, I wondered whether maybe I might borrow one for tonight?" I tried to sound super casual, but I failed.

"Oh, I get what this is about. You've brought some frumpy high-fashion thing to wear for dinner, and now you want something from your slutty friend's wardrobe because you've seen Cameron looks better than ever. And now you want to tempt him to lick you like ice cream on a hot sunny day and let's not even mention you melting and dripping down his cone."

"How DARE you suggest such a thing," I protested with the sort of grin that told her she was totally correct. "But... can I?"

"Tell you what, get us another round of cocktails, pick up the tab, and I'll let you have first pick of the dresses."

Chapter Two
Muriel Tennyson

Sandy, the receptionist, wasn't lying. Bruno worked miracles, and he tamed my hair so it fell in perfect loose waves around my shoulders.

I promised him a shoutout on my Instagram, but it didn't particularly interest him—apparently, he was already the worst kept secret for miles, with his calendar fully booked for the next six months. I'd been lucky to catch a last-minute cancellation. Apparently a client didn't want her hair done because of the weather forecast..

I sat in my bungalow with three dresses in front of me and Jasmine by my side. She had designed all three dresses herself; they were gorgeous. I was overthinking my outfit, but seeing Cameron had thrown me for a loop, and fashion always acted as my crutch when things became tricky.

"Go for the white one," Jasmine said confidently. "With your hair like that, you'll look like an angel."

I shook my head. "Chrissy said they're serving pasta tonight. I won't look like an angel, I'll look like a target. Tomato sauce, white fabric, and me are three things that do not go well together."

"Fair," Jas agreed. "So, two dresses left to choose from; floral or red. Do you want to go cute and flirty, or sexy and seductive?"

"Neither." I bit down on my bottom lip. "I just want to look... nice."

"The dress you brought is nice," Jas said, "but it's not going to get you laid. We both know what's happening here, so cut the crap and pick one."

Jasmine wouldn't fall for any false denials, so I gave in.

"Floral," I snapped. "Give me five minutes to finish getting ready, and we'll head over to the party."

In the bathroom, I changed into Jasmine's silk pink flower-covered dress. We were pretty much the same size, but it seemed I was slightly bigger in the bust, as the low-cut dress pressed tightly against my boobs.

In the mirror, I watched my breasts heave as I breathed, as though I was in a steamy period drama, which was exactly the sort of thing Jasmine designed costumes for. She was good at her job.

To tell the truth, I had no idea what I wanted from the evening. Seeing Cameron had given me a rush of excitement I hadn't experienced in a long time, and knowing Hugh was there too, made me even more nervous. But so much time had passed, and things had changed since we graduated high school; I didn't believe the spark would still be there for any of us.

Cameron had seemed relaxed when we met him earlier, but would he easily forgive me for ignoring and blocking him on social media? And what if we had nothing in common anymore?

Or, and this was the question that caused butterflies to dance a jig in my stomach, what if we still got along really, really well? Whatever the night had in store for me, I figured it would be best to be dressed to make a killer impression, just in case.

So I made some last-minute adjustments to my makeup and left the bathroom.

Jasmine wolf-whistled. "It fits you like a glove, Muriel. Cameron isn't going to know what hit him... or is it Hugh you're dying to see? You three were always so tight I couldn't work out which of them was the guy for you."

"Shut up," I said, rolling my eyes. My ears pricked as a horn honked outside. "Sounds like that's our cab."

My bungalow was in a beautiful location right by the lake, surrounded by large red cedar trees, but it was almost a mile from the event hall. Normally I'd enjoy the walk, but the weather had gotten even worse as the day turned to evening, and my rental car delivery had been delayed, although it was due any minute, so we ordered a cab. I intended to drink anyway, so I wouldn't have wanted to drive.

We arrived at the venue and ran inside to find Poppy waiting for us at the bar. The three of us grabbed drinks and walked through the hall, greeting old friends.

Chrissy had asked everyone she invited to let her know their favorite love song, and the playlist rang out around the venue.

I'd gotten chatting to someone whose face I recognized but couldn't quite place. He seemed to remember far more about me, increasing by the minute my discomfort at not even remembering his name.

"Yeah, my job's going pretty well," I replied to his question about my influencing work. "I really want to get into designing, but it's good for now. How about you, don't you work at—"

I had no idea what I would say next. I didn't want to seem like the sort of girl who's forgotten where she came from, but my brain seemed determined to lead me into a dead end.

"John, how's it going?"

With perfect timing, Cameron appeared at my side like a guardian angel. He gave me a subtle wink as he spoke to our old school friend. "How're things at the bakery?"

John, the baker, of course.

I remembered him. He always aced every test in home economics. I silently thanked Cameron for saving me, and I sneaked a glance at him, noting his dashing appearance in his slim-fit suit.

The two men began to discuss the thorny subject of croissants versus Danishes. I was about to join in when I caught a glimpse of Hugh across the hall, having what looked like a very intense conversation, but knowing him, it was probably small talk. He always had a way of making the most meaningless chat seem like the most important thing in the world, which probably helped him in his work as a journalist—people naturally opened up to him.

My heart hammered hard in my chest so fiercely I worried other people might hear it.

Hugh looked exactly as I imagined. He was easily the most underdressed person at the party in his worn jeans and a simple white shirt. Hugh never was the type to dress up on command. His curly black hair framed his face messily. It wouldn't have been my old friend if he'd obeyed the 'Glitz and Glam' dress code.

As I stole myself to go over and say hello, a bell rang out across the hall, interrupting my intentions. A waiter in a stuffy-looking suit stood on the small stage and asked us all to take our allocated seats. I scanned the room for Poppy and Jas, assuming I'd be sitting with them, until someone took me lightly by the elbow.

Cameron.

"I've got a suspicion we'll be sitting together," he said with a smile.

"And what makes you think that?"

Cameron shrugged. "I asked Vic to arrange it. I thought it'd be nice to catch up; you weren't exactly full of conversation this afternoon."

That was fair. I promised myself that I wouldn't get tongue-tied or carried away again for the rest of the night. Ladylike and dignified, that was my MO for the evening. I briefly wondered how Cameron managed to act as if nothing had happened between us after all this time, but then I remembered: *that's Cameron.*

He led me to a table beautifully laid with a white linen tablecloth and little glass vases filled with lavender and spearmint. Hugh was already seated when we arrived, and he stood to greet me.

"Muriel." Hugh stuck his hand out toward me like we were business associates meeting for the first time. If I didn't know him so well, I'd assume he hated me, but I happened to know he'd greet his mother the exact same way, so I shook his hand confidently.

Our table quickly filled up with more people I didn't recognize, although I assumed I should. I buried my disappointment that it wasn't only the three of us at the table.

As we all made small talk, the guys tactfully mentioned everyone's names, so I'd remember and not seem stuck up.

"So, I hear you're a big shot influencer now?" Hugh said once the general chatter died down.

"I wouldn't say big shot," I said, uncertain whether he intended it as a genuine question or a little dig at me. "It's a job, and it pays the bills."

"I'm a journalist at a local paper — the ability to pay bills is an alien concept to me."

There was that cynical, deadpan humor I loved. "It must be satisfying, though, getting to investigate local stories and break the news?"

Hugh shrugged, but as always, Cameron stepped in to brag on his behalf. "He single-handedly whipped the town council into shape with his reporting. Any hint of corruption or mismanagement, and he's on it like a hound dog."

"That's impressive," I said, genuinely glad that Hugh had found a career he loved. "I pose in front of graffiti-covered walls and say 'swipe up,' every now and again. Your job sounds a lot more fulfilling."

"Yeah, I guess so," Hugh conceded. "Although people always need escapism, and that's what you provide with your cute photos and everything."

That was a perspective I hadn't considered before; in my desperation to become a designer, I hadn't taken a moment to see what I actually did for a living in such a positive light.

"I mean, I assume the photos are cute," he continued, and I cringed, knowing what was coming next. "For some reason, I haven't found you on any social media."

Both guys raised their eyebrows while waiting for an answer, though I sensed they struggled to resist breaking out into grins. They were well aware that I'd blocked them, and I didn't want to have to explain myself, so I clapped my hands with glee when I was saved by the arrival of the waiter to serve our appetizers.

"Mmm, gazpacho," I exclaimed with more enthusiasm than necessary for a small bowl of soup.

We made it through the rest of the dinner without bringing up the fact that I'd removed them from my life again, and it started to seem like old times. We'd all grown in the past five years, but I still felt like we could be sitting in the library chatting excitedly about the future.

A waiter came round to top up the wine. Remembering my vow to be ladylike, I'd chosen white to avoid the dreaded purple teeth. The boys both chose red.

I stole a good glance at Hugh while the drink being poured distracted him; he had turned out to be a big old slice of heaven. Dark and brooding, his appearance fit his personality perfectly, just like Cameron's preppy, boyish looks suited him.

I remembered coming home from school and writing about both the guys in my diary. I'd make lists of pros and cons for each of them, trying to decide which one I'd want to date if they were interested. They were so different from each other, but the list always ended up even—they added up to the perfect man for me.

Lost in memories, I picked up my wine glass, brought it to my lips, and missed my mouth entirely. The rim bounced off my chin, sending a shower of alcohol down my neck and all over my dress. Ladylike and dignified: nailed it.

I pushed back my chair and leaped up, cheeks burning. But before I grabbed my napkin, Hugh was already there with his.

"You need to use sparkling water," he explained as I half-heartedly tried to stop him dabbing at my dress, "or the sugar in the wine will ruin the fabric."

"I can't believe I'm such a klutz."

"You're fine, don't worry about it," Cameron said as he joined Hugh in trying to clean me up.

I froze, remembering the last time I was sandwiched between them like this. It was too much; I excused myself and fled to the bathroom, with the excuse of needing to dry the dress.

I actually did the exact opposite. By splashing cold water on my face to calm down, I managed to soak the dress even more, but I was past caring. I simply had to hope it wasn't dry-clean only, or I'd owe Jasmine a bolt of fancy fabric at the very least.

Did the guys care about what happened between us back then? Did I care?

I stared at my flushed reflection in the mirror, trying to figure out how I felt.

It had started out as a bit of fun, really. Neither Hugh nor Cameron had been able to get dates for prom—which made no sense because they were clearly the hottest guys in school back then. I'd offered to talk to whichever girls had turned them down, but they refused to give me names, claiming they preferred to just hang out at Cam's house since his parents were away.

I'd been asked a couple of times, but not by *my* guys, so I didn't want to go. Instead, I asked if I could join in with their plans instead.

We'd decided to get dressed up as if we were going to prom, so I wore a slinky, blue, bias-cut gown. Of course, I had to wear a more modest dress over the top so my mom would let me out of the house, but that came off as soon as I was out of her sight.

The guys wore tuxes they'd rented, and they looked totally adorable.

At our exclusive prom for three, we listened to music and made weird cocktails with whatever we found in the house. We must have had ten times more fun than anyone at the actual prom.

"Hey, Muri," Hugh had said, fixing me with his intense glare that was more effective than CIA truth serum. "Which one of us is hotter?"

"Don't ask me that." I laughed, throwing a pillow at my friend.

"No, really, if you had to choose, who would it be?" Cam asked with a wicked glint in his eye.

The secret notes I'd made at home trying to compare the two only confirmed there was no answer; they were equally hot and equally perfect.

"You're equally gross." I'd lied and stuck my tongue out to lighten the mood.

They laughed, but then Hugh turned the music up and stood before me, holding my hand out like a gentleman in an old-fashioned romance novel. "Let's see who dances better, at least."

Dancing was the only thing we'd been missing from our prom night, so I couldn't refuse. Hugh and I started slow dancing to the romantic tones of *All About That Bass* by Meghan Trainor.

Obviously, we should have been laughing at the ridiculous situation, but as Hugh's hands slid from my upper to lower back, I tightened my grip around his neck. Goosebumps broke out all over my body, and for once, I felt like being completely serious.

We spun around the room for a couple of minutes, our bodies and faces getting closer and closer until I could hardly breathe. The song came to an end, along with a tap on my shoulder.

"My turn." Cameron grinned, and Hugh easily let me go and placed me in his friend's arms.

We danced slowly on the spot, swaying in time to a 1970s soul number.

Cameron let his fingers trail down my arm from my shoulder to my fingertips, then in a single smooth movement, he dipped me low and kissed me softly on the lips.

I kissed him back, gripping his arms tightly until he brought me back up to standing. We explored each other's mouths, tentatively at first but growing in confidence as we each realized the other was just as eager. I pressed my body against his and a hard bulge in his pants made me gasp with surprise and delight and fear.

After making out for a minute, the back of my neck tingled as Hugh placed light butterfly kisses on my skin. I almost bit Cameron's tongue in shock, but it felt so good I did nothing to stop him. In fact, I leaned back slightly, sandwiching myself in between these two men as they both explored me with their lips.

Cameron gently pulled away from me and turned me around so I faced Hugh, and then we began to kiss.

Hugh's kiss was harder than Cameron's, and he gripped my face as he ran his teeth playfully across my lower lip. I tucked my hands inside his suit jacket, pulling slightly at his shirt, and Cameron slowly began to lower the spaghetti straps of my dress.

"Stop!" I screamed as my brain finally managed to wrestle control of my body from my hormones. The guys both stopped immediately and stepped away respectfully.

"Are you all right, Muri?" Hugh had asked with concern written across his face. "Did we move too fast?"

"No, I mean yes, I mean... what did we just do? What was that?"

Cameron walked around so both young men stood in front of me, their gorgeous faces etched with concern.

"Didn't you want it?" Cameron asked, genuinely worried as I fanned my face in a vain attempt to calm down. "We thought you did."

"Want it? Want what? I'm a good girl, and I can't be doing that with two guys."

I still couldn't believe that my first kiss had turned out like that. At the time, I was so confused. My body, my heart, they liked it and wanted it to continue. But in my mind I just wondered how on earth the guys saw me as that kind of girl?

How could I have been so wild?

I wasn't the kind of girl who made out with two men at once; I'd been raised to not even agree to a date without checking with my parents first. What would they think of me if they found out what I'd done and what I desperately wanted to do?

Both guys moved forward to comfort me, but shame swelled in my stomach, and I batted them away.

"I have to go; I can't do this. I'm not like that."

I grabbed my coat and fled the house, using the time it took to walk back to my house to rationalize what had happened.

We'd all had too much to drink; it was just a bit of fun, nothing *really* happened. I was still a good girl, and I still only ever wanted to sleep with one guy in my life, certainly not two at one time. Not a chance.

It wasn't Cameron and Hugh's fault. At every turn, they behaved with respect, and deep down, I wanted it as much as they did. And that fact scared me so much.

Back then, I resolved to avoid them as much as possible; I'd be graduating soon, and I planned to move far away for college. I hoped my application to Savannah College of Art and Design would take me to Atlanta, so I wouldn't have to see the guys again.

Tears started to flow at the thought of not seeing my good friends, but it was for the best.

Someone entered the bathroom, snapping me out of my thoughts.

I glared at myself in the mirror. *You're not a naïve, sheltered girl anymore, Muriel,* I mouthed to my reflection. *You're a successful, experienced woman who can have whatever she wants. So, what do you want?*

Cameron, my mind answered. *And Hugh.*

Shit.

I headed back out to the dinner, which was just wrapping up and turning into a full-blown party.

"You two," I said to the guys as I approached, not bothering to sit down. "I'm going to head back to my bungalow. Do you want to come by later to catch up?"

It was a bold move, yes, and I still wasn't sure exactly what I expected to happen. It would be good to clear the air, just the three of us. Get over any lingering resentment over what had happened.

And if I had a real spark with either of them, I needed to figure it out. If it turned out I still had a spark with both of them, well, I would have to deal with that too.

I gave them the directions, then it still took me an age to get out of the door. I was pulled into conversation with half a dozen or more other guests and dancing with my friends. I have no idea how much later it was before I managed to leave, having lost track of time, but finally I said a quick goodbye to Poppy and Jas and headed out with a late night rendezvous in my mind.

Chapter Three
Cameron Moore

I couldn't stop smiling. Muriel had invited us back to her place. That had to be a good sign, right? At least it meant she didn't hate us, which is what we'd assumed all these years.

"She probably still hates us." Hugh had the uncanny ability to read my mind and then say the exact opposite thing.

"A woman wouldn't normally invite men she hates back to her hotel room." I countered as we climbed into my car. Even someone with Hugh's talent for pessimism couldn't argue with that.

"She would if... if she's planning to murder them," he replied eventually.

And I had to laugh. Hugh knew perfectly well Muriel had no intention of killing us; he just had to win this little battle of wits. Our shared sense of friendly competition that had kept us so close for all these years. Well, that and our shared love of women, although they were thin on the ground these days.

"Right, well, on the off-chance that we aren't about to die, how about we swing a small diversion and go by a liquor store first and pick up some schnapps and gin? We could even make those gross cocktails we had at our fake prom and try to recreate the mood."

Hugh's eyebrows disappeared somewhere high above his head. "You really think she wants to be reminded of the night she ran crying from your house? The night that made her ghost us both completely for five years?"

He had a point. I was about to turn the car around and head straight for her place when he continued, "We had Cool Ranch Doritos, too."

"So, you think it's worth a shot?"

"She's worth a shot, yes. A gentle, no-pressure shot. God knows we haven't met anyone else like her."

He wasn't wrong.

The night of the 'fake prom' provoked Hugh and me to talk at great length.

It turned into quite a confession. We both had the hots for Muriel, that was a given, and totally understandable. But we had more in common than just our desire for one girl.

I didn't think of myself as kinky or particularly wild, quite the opposite. I wanted to settle down with a lovely woman and raise kids in my hometown. But I also had fantasies about sharing my future wife with another man. Two men would surely please her twice as much as one and give her twice as much. It would be great to be a part of that set up.

All my sexual fantasies involved threesomes, I just couldn't help it.

I'd always wanted to be a small town cop and help my local community. So my secret desires were at odds with the person I thought I should be. Although those same desires were all about doing something to please my woman. I had no thoughts or intentions of having two people attend to me. The idea of a threesome with two women did nothing for me, I had no intention of trying it, and I wasn't into dudes, not it that way.

When I watched Hugh kissing Muriel, it was like I was on the very edge of all my dreams coming true and moments later, they were dashed.

It turned out that Hugh felt much the same way, and as we were already best buddies who enjoyed spending time together, it seemed natural enough that we should become increasingly comfortable with the idea of the two of us sharing a woman. It made sense to us.

But our efforts to date a woman together had not gone well. It seemed most women preferred one of us over the other, which isn't surprising since we were so different. And I do have to admit to a tiny jealous streak. Plus, Hugh always assumed the world was against him, so any arrangement we set up soon unraveled.

"She really did like us both back then, didn't she?" I voiced my inner thoughts as we drove to the store.

"Yes, she did." Hugh dreamily gazed out at the streetlights, which were blurred by drizzle on the windows. "And that night was hot."

"So hot." I agreed. "Hotter than a bunch of eighteen-year-old nerds had any right to be. The way she felt when pressed between us was just—" Hugh made a chef's kiss gesture.

I nodded heavily. "Exactly."

"But we fucked up. We pushed too hard. Stupid, horny teenagers that we were."

"Let's not dwell on that. She wants to see us now, and that's something."

We'd both done enough self-flagellating over what happened that night, and there wasn't any point in going over it again.

We pulled into the parking lot of a little late-night liquor store. "So; schnapps, gin, Coke, lemonade and Doritos. Anything else?"

"Alka-Seltzer? I don't think my stomach can handle all of that anymore." Hugh held his stomach dramatically until I punched him in the arm.

"You'll be fine; you're not fifty-three. Anyway, if the night goes like I hope, we'll be burning it off in no time." I jumped out of the car before Hugh had a chance to point out that I was being overly optimistic. "Back in a minute!" I called out before dashing away.

The truth was, I was more excited than I'd been in a long time, and I was sure that Muriel felt the exact same way from the expression on her face, the way she'd looked at us, and the fact that she'd invited us to her room Of course, I couldn't be certain, and I understood why Hugh was less confident.

Perhaps it was a sixth sense I'd developed with her from being friends for so long, or my natural ability to understand women, Or perhaps the fact that I totally caught her checking Hugh out right when she spilled her drink tonight gave me that boost in confidence. Either way, I practically danced around the store picking up the drinks and snacks we needed.

The rain came down even more heavily as we made our way over to her. I hoped it would pass before the wedding. Vic had mentioned they'd bought some brightly colored umbrellas to use as props if needed, so perhaps a rainy-day wedding would be cute after all.

Raindrops battered the windscreen as I got back into the car and handed the plastic bags over to Hugh.

"Hold these," I said and turned on the ignition. "I'm taking us to our girl."

"She's not ours y—" Hugh began, but I held up a finger and wagged it at him as I drove out the parking lot.

"Not another word from you unless it's a positive one. Now, cheer up and look forward to swigging that schnapps."

We didn't talk for the remainder of the short drive.

I drove carefully in the stormy weather, so it took a while to reach Muriel's place. There was no parking directly outside, so we used a lot a hundred yards up the road and ran to her front door. It was just far enough to ensure we were soaked through like a pair of drowned rats when we arrived on her porch.

I knocked on the door, and for a minute, there was no answer.

"The lights are all off," Hugh said, peering through the small window by the door. "I guess she's gone to bed."

"I'll just knock one more time," I said, not wanting to wake her if she had changed her mind, but also not wanting to give up on this reunion.

I raised my fist, but before I knocked again, Muriel opened the door, and I gasped at the sight of her.

She'd changed out of her dress and wore a pair of black yoga pants and a simple white tank top. She'd tied her hair back loosely, revealing her slender neck, and curls fell adorably around her face.

"Sorry guys, I was just getting changed," she explained. "Come on in."

I gave Hugh a quick *I-told-you-so* look before following her into the bungalow.

"Nice place," Hugh said, admiring the cozy and tastefully decorated living room.

"Isn't it lovely? It's three times the size of my apartment in LA," Muriel replied. "And it would probably cost about a tenth of the price to buy."

"Sounds like someone's ready to move back here," I half-joked.

I put the groceries on the coffee table and tried to suppress a shiver. The rain had soaked through the light fabric of my suit, and the coldness clung to my skin.

"Oh, look at you both." Muriel rushed over to help Hugh out of his denim jacket that looked like it had shrunk in the two minutes we were outside.

When I noticed that she took her time taking the jacket off him, I couldn't help but smile.

Her hands lingered on his shoulders, and her face moved just slightly too close to his body to be completely innocent.

I also couldn't help noticing her incredible ass as she stood on her tiptoes; yoga pants are truly God's gift to man. I shrugged off my suit jacket and my shirt had turned see-through from the water.

"I look like I'm in a nineties boy band video," I joked, unable to resist gyrating my hips rhythmically to some non-existent pop music. Hugh and Muriel laughed at me, and I beamed with joy from having our little group back together again.

"Would you believe it? This place has two bathrooms," Muriel said, pointing toward a small corridor beyond the kitchen area. "Why don't you both get showered? I'm sure there are some robes in the closet through there, too."

"Perfect." I said. "And while we're doing that, why don't you rummage through those grocery bags? I hope you like what we've brought."

"As long as it's unhealthy, I'll be happy." Muriel peered into the bags with interest. "I'm sick to death of avocados and vegan protein bars."

"Welcome back to Georgia, then." Hugh grinned as he pulled out the giant bag of Doritos I'd bought.

Muriel's face lit up, and she grabbed them from him. "Hurry up and get your showers, and we can dig in."

***

The hot shower left me energized despite it being almost midnight. I normally worked early shifts with Vic, but luckily I had the weekend off since Vic was off as well and it was his wedding.

Being awake after ten seemed decadent, especially wrapped in a fluffy white robe and about to catch up with the woman of my dreams.

I strode back into the living room, feeling on top of the world, and found Hugh already showered and wearing an identical robe.

"Hey." Muriel said, "Come and join us. I was just saying, those spirits you got were very thoughtful, but also kind of disgusting all together, so I thought wine might be more our speed?"

It was Hugh's turn to mouth, *I told you so,* at me, but I just brushed it off. Given that we were both practically naked, the evening was going well, regardless.

"How about a game of strip poker?" I suggested, and both of my friends quirked their brows. "I mean, Hugh and I can only lose once with what we're wearing, but—no? You sure?"

Muriel nodded, but she was trying not to smile.

"Okay, your loss. How about..."

I sorted through the pile of games the resort provided, stacked up next to the TV. Most were the typical boring games; Monopoly, Scrabble, chess. Hugh would probably love that. Although, would strip chess work? *No, Cameron*, I told myself, leave the whole '*Strip*' genre alone, for now at least. I'd almost given up when I spotted the perfect game at the bottom of the pile.

"Truth or Dare." I asked over my shoulder; Muriel appeared interested, but Hugh wore a disdainful expression.

"Sure, why not?" Muriel said, which prompted Hugh to shrug his acceptance.

Perfect.

"Right, we all take turns drawing a card and ask the person clockwise to us whether they want a truth or a dare. So, Muriel, what'll it be," I asked as I shook the contents from the box.

"I'll go dare, please."

I shuffled the cards before turning the top one over.

"Call up a Chinese restaurant and order a pizza."

"Um, no," she replied, to my relief. "Isn't that a bit mean? Wasting their time and all."

"That is... the right answer." I adopted my game-show host voice. "So, truth then?"

She waved her hand for me to proceed and took a big gulp of wine.

"What is your biggest fantasy?" Oh, nice one; this was truly the perfect game.

Muriel's cheeks reddened slightly, but she was determined not to bow out of the game at the first question, so she scratched her chin thoughtfully. "I'd like to... have sex in Paris."

"That's not a fantasy," Hugh said. "That's just a thing French people do."

"Well, I'm not French, am I?" she pointed out. "It was a question for me, and I'm not using phone-a-friend, so you can shut your yap."

Wow, things were getting spicy already. Hugh tried to appear offended, but I knew full well he liked being put in his place by a strong woman.

"Paris it is, then," Hugh said. "Right, you pull a card for Cameron now."

"Okay. Cameron, truth or dare?"

"Given the quality of the last dare, I think we'll make this game truth or truth. So, truth, please."

"What's something you're glad your dad doesn't know about you?"

I didn't even have to take a second to think about my answer. "Nothing. I'm an open book, he already knows everything."

"Seriously, everything?" Hugh asked. "I did not know that strange and slightly disturbing fact."

"We can't all be an international man of mystery, life you are." He told his parents as little as possible about his life. His relationship with his family was a stark contrast to mine.

"That's admirable," Muriel said, and I nodded my appreciation. "Absolutely nutso, but admirable."

"Agreed. And onward, I've got a truth for you, Muriel," Hugh said, and while she gestured for him to go ahead, I eyed him warily. He'd been in a weird mood ever since Muriel invited us over, and I didn't trust him not to ruin the mood. Was he going to ask her for her views on Ukraine? Or where she was on her menstrual cycle?

"Why *did* you ghost us?"

Oh.

That.

I'd have taken Ukraine over that.

It took every ounce of strength in me to resist literally facepalming. You can always trust a journalist to suck the fun out of a party. Although I wouldn't deny that I was interested to hear the answer to his question. But his timing sucked; he really didn't need to do it when things were just getting flirty.

Chapter Four
Muriel Tennyson

Fairy lights adorned the walls of the bungalow living room, giving a soft, radiant glow. I'd put some smooth lo-fi hip hop on, lit a sandalwood candle, and generally made the place as relaxing and low-key sexy as possible.

Truth or Dare, or Truth or Truth as it turned out, was fun.

And then Hugh rolled in with the one question guaranteed to kill the mood.

"Why *did* you ghost us?"

I was on the spot, no time to make anything up. Assuming the game portion of the evening had ended, I busied myself putting the cards away, giving my eyes something to focus on other than their faces.

"I was scared."

"Scared of what?" Cameron asked, more gently than Hugh's probing question. But he was clearly very interested. As he leaned forward, his robe rode up his leg, revealing a muscular thigh. I swallowed hard.

"I was a virgin, for crying out loud." I threw my hands in the air in a mock-dramatic move. "Nobody expects their first time to be a threesome, do they?"

Hugh nodded and wagged his finger enthusiastically as if he finally got it. "She has a point."

"Damn right, I have a point," I said, slightly annoyed that it hadn't occurred to them before now. "So I ran away. I was ashamed of how much I wanted it too even though I thought it was wrong. And I blocked you on my social media because..."

"Because you didn't want to see us with other women." Hugh's assessment was accurate, but I didn't want them to know that.

"Hah. Don't flatter yourselves. I wanted a fresh start, that's all, away from this place and everyone I knew. Jasmine, Poppy, and I all agreed that we'd become new people in college, and that's what we did."

Cameron seemed satisfied with that explanation, but Hugh's expression seemed doubtful. His dark, intelligent eyes searched my own until he finally decided against probing any further.

"Anyway. We're all back together now. And I'm so happy you're both doing what you love. Remember how we'd talk about you two becoming the dream team of a cop and investigative journalist? You're living that dream, aren't you?"

"Oh, I loved it when we all huddled together in the library. And I guess we have all made it, more or less. Although, Hugh should be applying for jobs at the New York Times, or Reuters or something rather than wasting his talents on a small town paper."

My heart glowed knowing that Cameron remembered those chats that meant so much to me.

"I've got some contacts at the Los Angeles Times. If you want, I could probably get you an interview." An old boyfriend of mine was some sort of entertainment editor there, but I didn't want to tell him that part. I took a long sip of my delicious wine, which came from a welcome basket in the bungalow.

Hugh didn't even pause before shaking his head vigorously, sending his wet curly bangs bouncing adorably across his forehead. "Thanks, but I like being a big fish in a small pond. I can get actual results here, and my editor gives me the freedom to investigate whatever I like. At a bigger paper, I'd have to satisfy advertisers and avoid offending anyone."

I nodded with genuine understanding. "Yes, I can see why avoiding causing offense would be difficult for you."

Hugh had a heart of gold, but his no-nonsense way of talking definitely pissed off people who expected to be treated with kid gloves.

"Can you go to my parent's house and explain that to my mom then, please? She thinks I should be on CNN or something, and she can't understand why I care so much about local land zoning issues."

To be honest, I didn't understand why Hugh would care about land zoning either. It sounded like the most boring topic on earth. But his unwavering passion for justice and fairness fascinated me, so it was best to encourage whatever sparked his interest.

"Hmm, yes, land zoning," I adopted what I hoped was a thoughtful tone. "A very important issue."

He grinned knowingly. "You don't know what land zoning is, do you?"

"Nope," I said, laughing, and Hugh threw a small handful of chips at me in response. "What? I'm a mere fashion influencer; I don't have to know anything about that kind of thing."

We sat for a minute in comfortable silence, eating chips and drinking, until the question that had been playing on my mind all evening finally burst from my lips. "So, any girlfriends?"

"We're single at the moment," Hugh replied swiftly.

I watched carefully as they glanced at each other, and Hugh gave Cameron the nod to say something further. I braced myself to find out just how wise I'd been to avoid looking at their Instagram.

"There's not been many, really," Cameron said, and I released a breath I didn't know I'd been holding. "Nothing long-term at all. The most serious one was probably Hannah, but she turned out to be a bit crazy, so—"

"Wait." I held my hand up, stopping him mid-sentence. "Not Hannah Decker?" It was a small town; how many twenty-something Hannahs could there be?

"Yup," Hugh said through gritted teeth, squeezing his eyes shut as if trying to block out a terrible memory. "She seemed nice at first, but when she didn't get a proposal within two months of dating, she started getting weird. Leaving printouts from jewelers' sites in the car, changing my ringtone to *Here Comes the Bride.* Really nuts."

An admittedly unreasonable ball of anger formed in my stomach. "Well, I could have told you she was nuts. She played volleyball for Rothbury High, and when we played against her, she broke into our changing room and cut up all our uniforms."

"Yikes," Cameron said.

"Exactly."

I couldn't believe my mortal enemy had dated Hugh. Or was it Cameron? He'd made it sound that way. "So, did you date her, Hugh?" I asked while I topped up our wine and re-filled the chip bowl. It was almost one in the morning, and we had a wedding the next day, but I was having too much fun learning about my guys to even consider going to bed.

"We both did, together," Hugh answered.

They both dated Hannah?

"So whoever dated her first didn't warn the other, or whoever dated her second didn't believe the warning?"

"No. Nothing like that. We both dated her at the same time."

She got the experience I should have had? My blood ran cold.

"Oh." I tried to sound unshaken, but my voice cracked, despite my only uttering a single syllable.

"You must have realized that was something we were into," Cameron said gently, leaning toward me from the other couch. "After what happened that night."

"Yes, I get it," I replied, conscious that I sounded slightly hysterical. *Calm down, Muriel,* I told myself. *They're entitled to a past, just like you are; even though yours is somewhat boring compared to theirs.* "It's just the thought of you two with Hannah, it's... hard for me to think about."

"I understand," Cameron said.

Hugh put his arm around my shoulder comfortingly. I was tempted to push him away, but my heart overruled my brain, and I leaned my head against his firm chest.

"In fairness, it's not exactly easy to find women who are into, well, our lifestyle in this small town," Hugh explained. "We've tried dating a couple of other women, but they didn't work out either. They were all nice enough; they just weren't..."

"They weren't you." Cameron finished Hugh's sentence.

The words hung in the air as I tried to process what they'd just revealed.

A number of conflicting feelings swirled around inside me, but the one that overwhelmed me ultimately was attraction. I was incredibly attracted to both of these men, and knowing that they had been pining for me like I'd longed for them had the strangest effect on me. I summoned courage from the wine and placed a hand on Hugh's thigh.

"I've had boyfriends; only one at a time, mind you. But none of them were you," I admitted, and I watched both of their expressions change from awkward to joyous as they heard what I'd said.

"You mean, you do like us? Both of us?" Cameron asked, nodding at me in encouragement.

Hugh said nothing, but he placed a large, strong hand over mine and lightly held it in place.

The slight touch and the words I was about to say made my heart beat harder.

"Both of you," I barely whispered my confession.

Chapter Five
Muriel Tennyson

Somewhere in the back of my brain, a voice screamed at me to put a stop to this, to ask them to leave and never see them again. A three-way relationship would never work out; how could it? The word is couple, not throuple.

It would have to be a secret; my career in the public eye would be over in a heartbeat if anyone found out. And if it lasted long enough, I would never, ever be able to bring them both home to my family for Christmas, not unless I wanted to kill my poor mother. I may not be an innocent young woman anymore, but that didn't mean I would accept being talked about as a freak by relatives and strangers alike.

And yet, I had just told Cameron and Hugh the truth. I wanted both of them, and they were both here right now, in front of me, looking like they wanted to devour me in the hottest possible way.

Would one night together hurt?

"Muriel," Hugh said, "we want you, too. We've never wanted anyone else. The moment we were old enough to notice girls, we noticed you, and that was it."

"For both of us," Cameron added. "We're yours."

Holy moly, was it getting hot in that bungalow? I fanned myself as I tried to decide between two options. It was either give in to my fear and ask them to leave. or give in to my desire and ask them to stay the night. Whichever way it went, there was no going back.

Fuck it.

"And I'm yours," I said.

And Cameron pounced on me like a wildcat.

In less than a moment, I was in his arms, and I managed to wrap my legs tight around his waist at the same time as he planted a hot, passionate kiss on my lips.

I kissed him back greedily, not caring about how desperate I appeared. I *was* desperate; this was long overdue.

While we kissed, a series of little butterfly kisses on the back of my neck, and they were a bigger nostalgia trigger than any gross cocktail might have been.

Hugh, my Hugh, the cynical, world-weary gumshoe, treated me with such tenderness that it almost made my heart explode. His hands slowly reached round to cup my breasts, at first over and then under my shirt.

Cameron kept kissing me like his life depended on it, while gripping my ass fiercely.

"To the bedroom," Hugh breathed.

Cameron acted in the instruction and began to walk without breaking our connection for a second.

My mind briefly wandered to the logistics of what was about to happen, and I didn't plan to stop it. I had no idea how any of it would work; were there rules? Etiquette? What positions were there for two guys and a girl?

Relax, I told myself as I moaned with desire into Cameron's mouth. These guys knew what they were doing, and they cared about me. For one night only, let myself go and enjoy it.

It only took a few of Cameron's long strides to take us through to the bedroom, where I dropped my legs to the floor. As our torsos pressed together, Cameron's erection pressed against his robe, and I looked down to find the biggest tent I'd ever seen. Until I turned around, that is, and there stood Hugh with an equally large bulge in his robe. I stood between them like a rabbit in the headlights, not sure what to do next.

"It's okay," Hugh said, stepping close to me and stroking my cheek gently. "We've got this."

Cameron's fingers slipped under the straps of my tank top, and this time I didn't tell him to stop. I lifted my arms as he ever so slowly pulled the top from my body, leaving me standing half-naked in front of Hugh.

"Beautiful," he breathed, but he didn't move a muscle.

Cameron moved to my yoga pants, pulling them down in a slow, smooth movement, removing my panties with them. He remained behind me while Hugh continued to gaze at my deliciously exposed body as though admiring a piece of art in a gallery. His studious attention only turned me on even more. I was ready to climax on the spot.

But this wasn't enough, I needed to see the guys naked, too.

"Well, come on then, catch up, you two." I laughed, not wanting to lose the fun from our relationship just because we were finally getting it on.

Hugh stepped away from me. "Come and get me, then," he teased, so I did exactly that.

I walked over to him and untied his robe, letting it fall to the floor around his feet. He looked magnificent. I'd underestimated the guy; I didn't expect someone so deep and serious would be interested in the gym, but he clearly worked out *hard*.

My skin goose-bumped, and my nipples hardened as I took in every inch of his sculpted body, from his broad, muscular shoulders to his thick, delicious calves.

I wasn't the frightened inexperienced virgin any more. I knew what I wanted and how much the sight of him standing there like that turned me on. My whole body hummed with arousal.

Of course, I spared several seconds to lustfully admire his cock, which stood out proudly from his body, tempting me to reach out and touch it.

So I did.

I took his cock in my hand, gingerly at first, and started to stroke his length. He groaned, a low and animalistic moan, and I almost couldn't believe this was happening. Not with Hugh, *my* Hugh, one of the men I'd been dreaming about and thought I'd lost forever, groaning at my touch.

I started to pump harder until another cock pressed gently against my ass. The other star of my dreams.

Cameron pressed his body close to mine and began to massage my breasts. He pinched and teased my nipples until I cried out, and he covered my neck with strong, determined kisses.

I writhed against him, making sure that I didn't stop pleasuring Hugh with my hand.

He did the same for me in return, placing one hand on my hip while the other explored my outer lips, using his fingers to stroke and find his way into my most intimate area. He used his thumb to tap my clit, and I jumped, shocked by the almost electric current of pleasure that ran through me.

"You're so sensitive," Cameron purred into my ear. "If I guess you've wanted this for a long time too, would I be right?"

"Yes," I whispered, and he continued to play with my breasts while Hugh deftly worked his magic fingers between my thighs.

I'd imagined this very moment a thousand times, but I never knew how overwhelmingly good it would feel to have four hands all devoted to my pleasure.

My orgasm quickly reached its crescendo, and my knees buckled as it crashed through me. Hugh held me against him, and I whimpered and moaned into his chest as wave upon wave of pure bliss swept through my whole body. Finally, the sensation began to subside, and Hugh steadied me on my feet with a warm, slightly goofy smile.

"That good?"

"Good?" I spluttered. "I'm going to need you to do that to me every day for the rest of our lives. My God, that's the hardest I've ever come in my life."

"Well, I'm going to have to break that record, aren't I?" Cameron's ever-so-slightly jealous tone made me laugh; I should have figured these guys would even be competitive in the bedroom.

Cameron swept me off my feet and laid me down on the bed. He stood in front of it and eyed me like a ravenous carnivore might stare at its dinner.

Any other time being exposed and examined like that by a guy from school would have seemed so embarrassing. But right then, I felt both beautiful and sexy in a dirty sluttish sort of way.

My best friends had unpicked my inhibitions and were honing in on all the things that truly turn me on.

For a few seconds I wondered what would happen next, what did they plan to do with me? Soon, Cameron pushed my legs wide apart, fell to his knees in between, and moved his face so close to my intimate place and his warm breath wafted over me.

"You look so good, Muriel. I want to savor every minute. I can't wait to taste you, but I'm enjoying the anticipation too."

His words made me whimper a little as I suppressed a moan.

Could he actually make me come without touching me? It was already close.

That suppressed moan didn't stay trapped inside me for long.

Cameron's gentle, wet, warm tongue swirled around my clit and then darted between my sensitive folds.

His hands on my thighs held me in place as if he knew his actions would make me squirm and writhe if possible.

I glanced over at Hugh, wondering about his intentions.

He appeared perfectly content to watch my face for every reaction. Not just content, though. Turned on by it. My gaze scanned down to see him rubbing himself as he thoroughly enjoyed the sexy show from his position. He had his own close-up live, private, porny sex show. And one that he was welcome to join in at any time.

How did I ever find myself becoming part of something like this? I didn't have an answer. I was discovering something new about sex, and the woman I could be, and I loved it.

I loved it so much that when he entered me with his fingers, I couldn't hold back. I didn't want to. It was as if Cam urged me on, flicked a switch, and sent me over the edge of the cliff.

The orgasm crashed through me as if it were a tangible physical beast knocking all the wind right out of me and leaving me breathless.

Then, in one swift movement, he had my legs hoisted over his shoulders; I was suddenly grateful for all the time and money I'd spent on yoga classes.

Like a well organized tag team, Hugh handed over a condom and my man Cam was suited up and ready to go

His cock was perfectly poised against my entrance, and I let out an involuntary moan as he teased me with his hesitation.

Cameron chuckled. "I guess that means you're ready?"

"Yes. Oh God, fuck me, Cameron, fuck me." I couldn't believe the words that came out of my mouth. I'd never experienced such a sense of abandon before; nobody had made me want to beg, but at that moment, I needed Cameron more than I needed air.

The head of his cock pressed into me, and it felt so good that I almost blacked out. My body stretched to take him in, and it was just on the right side of painful as he took his time entering me inch by heavenly inch.

I threw my head back when he finally reached his limit, and I cried out in desperate need.

He started to thrust, slowly at first and then picking up speed until he hit a perfect rhythm.

"Hugh?" I panted, "Where are you?" This needed to be a true three-way, and while I was sure he was enjoying the show, I wanted both of my men to be involved.

"I'm here, Muri," Hugh said, and he was by my side, kneeling on the bed.

He was still rock hard, so I continued where I left off, stroking and pumping his cock until he came with a howl, spraying his hot white seed all over my stomach. I didn't stop until he'd spilled every last drop; I loved seeing how happy I made this serious man.

Once he'd recovered from his orgasm, Hugh leaned down and kissed me with surprising tenderness; the sensation contrasted sharply to the unyielding pace that Cameron fucked me. The combination was enough to make me come again, hard, and I gasped while bucking my hips desperately in the air.

As my climax began to recede, Cameron's arrived, and he gave one last powerful thrust as he came. The expression of pure lust on his face almost sent me over the edge again.

Eventually, Cameron pulled out, disposed of the condom, and joined us on the bed.

We lay together, naked on top of the covers; three old friends who had done something amazing together. I wanted to stay awake and talk to them all night long, but exhaustion overtook me, and I soon fell into a dreamy sleep, wrapped in my lovers' arms.

Chapter Six
Hugh Davis

It had been the most wonderful night of my life, but as I watched her sleep between Cam and me, the inevitable fact that it wouldn't happen again weighed heavily on me. The magical intimacy had to come to an end. It wouldn't last. Nothing that good ever lasted long.

She's going to regret it.

"Wasn't that amazing?" Cameron whispered.

I wouldn't expect him to understand. He always expected everything to work out well. He even thought Hannah would be a good match for us, although more due to desperation combined with optimism than genuine belief.

I didn't have his ability to block out the cold, hard facts. And in this case the fact was Muriel had moved on from our town and from us. One night of mind-blowing hot sex wasn't going to change that.

"Let's go into the living room," I whispered back at Cameron.

We put on our robes and tucked Muriel into bed; she was out cold. I couldn't help but admire her beautiful body while trying not to perve, certain it was the last time I'd ever see it.

"So, what do you think?" Cameron excitedly asked once we'd made our way to the living room and shut the doors. "You've heard the well known saying, women always want more of Cameron Moore."

I snorted. Perhaps I shouldn't have, but honestly, where could this go? Why would an LA influencer with ambition move back to Georgia? To be in a three-way relationship with a small-time cop and an even smaller-time journalist? Unlikely.

"Don't laugh," Cameron said with a frown. "She likes us, otherwise why would she have done what she just did?"

I shrugged. "Experimentation? Curiosity? For the fun of it? Wanted to get something out of her system?"

My suggestions were obviously more reasonable than Cam's dreams. And he thought so too, judging by how his face changed from annoyed to worried.

"Okay, we've had one incredible night with her; that's more than we ever expected, so let's not worry about the future right now."

"You're right," Cameron agreed, although his tense features suggested he wanted to argue. "I need to start helping Vic get ready at eight and it's so late already, I'd better get some sleep. I noticed spare sheets in the bedroom. I'll grab them, and we can sleep on these couches."

I fell asleep, wondering how we would all handle the wedding. If Muriel did end up regretting our night together, it would be horribly awkward, and Cameron and I would have to keep a respectful distance from her. But keeping Cameron under control was sometimes like trying to train a puppy. I'd have to take care of him and his feelings like I always did.

Not long after I finally drifted off to sleep, an enormous crash woke me up with a start. It seemed like the world was ending, and that effect was only heightened by the fact that only inky darkness surrounded us. All the electricity had gone off.

"What's happening?" Muriel shouted as she stumbled out of the bedroom. "I thought I was having a nightmare."

She carefully made her way into our room and over to Cameron, who put a reassuring arm around her shoulder.

"I guess it's something to do with the storm." I stood up to fetch my phone from my still-soaked jeans.

I switched the flashlight on and scanned the room, it all looked the same as it did before we went to sleep.

Outside was a different matter, and through the glass panel in the door and the window beside it our problem quickly became clear. An enormous tree lay on its side right outside the front door. It wasn't there when we arrived. It had evidently collapsed in front of the bungalow, taking down the lines outside as well as blocking our exit.

"Is there another way out?" I asked.

"Yes. There's a patio area down the hall there."

"You stay here, and I'll go check it out."

While I investigated an alternative exit, I left them in darkness, comfortable enough, huddled together and still half asleep.

It didn't take long.

"The patio doors have been sealed shut, and, well, that's illegal," I reported back.

Cameron glared at me.

"What? It's true." *Don't blame the messenger.*

"It's also not very helpful right now. What are we going to do?"

Though barely awake, I tried to come up with a plan. "We should definitely try to get out if we can. We don't know whether that tree has affected the structure of this place. The whole place might come crashing down."

"Oh, god," Muriel moaned, and Cameron's arm shot around her again.

He gave me an exasperated icy stare, which was fair. This probably wasn't the time for my particular brand of realism.

"Don't worry, I'm just being, you know, me," I said, making her laugh as I tilted her chin up to look at me. "You understand what I'm like."

"I know you're an idiot," she grumbled.

"You're scared, so I'll accept that. Right, my phone isn't working; the storm must have affected things. Cameron, do you have your radio with you?"

He nodded and headed over to his clothes to find it.

"Officer Moore here," he spoke into his radio, his voice still rough from sleep. "Is anybody there?"

"Officer Moore, this is Officer Price."

"Vic. Oh God, I'm sorry for waking you so early on your wedding day—"

We all caught the bitter edge to the laughter that came through the radio. "You didn't wake me, Cameron, and this isn't my wedding day anymore. Haven't you noticed? All hell has broken loose."

I loved my best friend so much; no other person on earth would get trapped in a house by a storm, assume that was the only damage, and still expect a wedding to go ahead at the exact same resort a few hours later. I had to admit I was sometimes jealous of his extreme optimism, even if it did make him seem a bit silly sometimes.

"Of course, of course," Cameron stammered, "I'm sorry about that. But this is the problem, we're in one of the bungalows at Lakeview, and a tree has fallen in front of it, so we can't get out. Any chance someone can get down here and help us?"

"They can, but it won't be for a while. This storm has hit hard, and we're stretched thin. If you can get out the window, that's probably your best option."

I went over to one of the windows to check the opening. Muriel would fit, but it would be tight for Cam and me. We'd have to completely strip off to avoid any clothes getting caught and hope we didn't get stuck.

They obviously had in mind that the entrance door and the patio doors were the emergency exits when they designed the place.

"What about if we try smashing the patio door?" Cameron suggested, but I shook my head.

"The storm's still raging. If our car won't start for some reason and we smash up this place, we'll be stuck without shelter unless we make a dash to the hotel. We'll probably be safer staying right here." It was a bit of a turnabout from saying the place might be about to come crashing down around our ears, but I'd had a moment to calm down and get my brain working rationally.

"He's got a point there, Cameron," Vic said, and even in the circumstances, I couldn't resist giving my friend a little smirk. "You guys hang tight, and we'll get you out as soon as possible. Is it only you and Hugh?"

"Um, and Muriel," Cameron said, and a long silence followed on the other end of the radio.

"Interesting," Vic said finally, and I detected a note of amusement in his voice. "Well, I hope you've got supplies and some form of entertainment, because you're probably going to be there a while."

"Understood. Over and out." Cameron put down his radio.

"So, we're stuck?" Muriel's lower lip quivered and her eyes welled up with tears. I wanted to comfort her, but I might have been the reason she was so upset.

"You can leave if you like," I pointed out mildly. "You can fit through the window and maybe try to get over to the main hotel."

She appeared to consider it for a moment but ultimately shook her head. "No, I'm not abandoning you. We'll ride this thing out together."

"Excellent." Cameron clapped his hands together happily.

I knew exactly the way his mind worked; he believed she chose to stay with us because she liked us. He imagined us heading straight back to the bedroom to ride out this storm by riding her. That was the optimistic spirit I admired.

"What shall we do then?"

"Well, it's still basically the middle of the night," Muriel pointed out. "I don't know about you, but I'm going to try to get some more sleep."

My friend deflated before my eyes. "Oh. I just thought that maybe we might—"

"We'll talk in the morning, all right?" Muriel interrupted him and headed back to her bedroom before either of us could say anything else.

"Don't you dare say I told you so," Cameron hissed.

I had to laugh. Just like I could read his mind, he knew me like the back of his hand, too. "Fine, I'll resist, just this once."

We made our way back over to our respective couches. It wasn't like I was happy with being right. I didn't enjoy her reticence. If she'd torn my clothes off and dragged me back to her bed, I'd have been delighted to admit I was wrong. But Cameron would be so much more disappointed than me. Being a cynic before my time meant I was better prepared for life's letdowns.

The wind continued to batter against the windows as I fell into a fitful sleep.

Chapter Seven
Muriel Tennyson

I didn't go back to sleep, despite saying I intended to. I was too restless, turning everything over in my mind. The truth was, I didn't know what to say to the guys. Thanks for last night? Too cheesy. Let's do it again? Tempting, but asking for trouble. What the hell do we do now? That was the question I really wanted to ask, but I wasn't sure any answer existed that would make us all happy.

So instead of sleeping, I stared at the ceiling, or at least the pitch-black darkness that hung in the air between me and the ceiling.

What a mess I'd gotten myself into. The wedding would have been awkward enough, but instead we'd ended up trapped together in a bungalow.

Vic knew the guys stayed with me overnight, so it wouldn't be long before the whole town found out about it. What would everyone think? I'd have to say that their car broke down after giving me a lift.

But then, if the guys had shared women before—and the thought of that made me ill—perhaps everyone already knew about that, so they'd just assume I was their latest conquest. Which was true, but I didn't need everyone to find out about it. What if my parents found out? I usually wasn't a neurotic person, but this combination of friendship, lust, and small-town gossip seemed custom-made to stress me out.

Eventually, I must have fallen asleep because suddenly, pure post-storm sunlight bathed the pale cream room.

The smell of coffee lured me into the kitchen like a moth to a flame.

"Found a French press," Hugh waved the appliance at me. "We're on our second round. Cream?"

"No, thanks," I said with a smile.

He poured three cups of tar-black coffee. I added some sugar and took my cup over to the bookshelf in the living room, looking for a way to pass the time without having to talk to the guys too much.

The guys were both still in their robes, which I found annoying because it reminded me so much of what we did last night. Their clothes were still damp, so they didn't have much choice, but my irrational mind responded with irritation while my impulsive body responded to their disheveled appearance in a different way.

I blushed, remembering how I'd begged them as the two guys explored my body. It was like I'd been possessed; I'd never behaved that way in front of another person before. And now I would have to spend the day with them, pretending none of it had happened in order to keep my head clear and decide what to do next.

"Have any of you read *The DaVinci Code*?" I asked, and they answered at the same time.

"Amazing."

"Fucking terrible."

I laughed. If they'd given those answers anonymously, I could have guessed who'd said what.

My tastes were more aligned with Hugh's than Cameron's, so I put the book back on the shelf.

Ah, an old copy of Emma by Jane Austen; perfect.

I pulled it from the shelf and headed over to an armchair in the corner of the room.

"So, Muriel," Cameron said in his small-talk voice. "Tell me, what exactly is an influencer?"

It was a fair question and one which people often asked me. Hugh understood what I did for a living, but Cameron was practically a Luddite, preferring to avoid all but the essential aspects of the internet.

"It's just someone who... influences people, I guess. To buy things."

"So, like a sales rep?"

I bobbed my head noncommittally. "Kind of, only I don't directly sell things. Brands pay me to take photos of their products because I make them look good, so people will want to buy them."

"So, like a store mannequin?"

My instinct was to argue back, but Cameron had asked the question so innocently, and it was a reasonable comparison, so I bit my tongue. "Sure. I'm a walking, talking mannequin. Well, actually, it's a bit like product placement in a favorite TV series or an advertorial in a newspaper."

"Great. And you can do that sort of work anywhere, can you?"

The hairs on the back of my neck prickled; this man had an agenda, and I wasn't going to fall for it.

"Pretty much, although it helps if you live somewhere photogenic. But I don't enjoy influencing, to be honest. It pays the bills, but I see it as a stop-gap. What I really want to do is start my own line of clothing, kind of like what Jasmine does now, only with mainstream clothes instead of cosplay stuff."

"And that can be done anywhere, too?" Cameron asked, a touch too casually for my liking.

"Nah, at least to start off, I'd probably have to be based in fashionable LA or New York," I replied, although that wasn't true at all.

My dream was to start a label somewhere small and unusual, somewhere with a small-town hometown kid of a vibe. It would be a unique selling point, and I would use the local area for inspiration to make clothes unlike what you see in the fashion capitals. Start-up costs would be lower too; I'd done the math, so I knew how to make it work. I just didn't have the actual funds yet.

His face fell on hearing my answer, and I felt bad, but I wasn't in the right headspace to talk about anything serious right now. All I wanted was to get lost in Austen, get rescued, and then have some time to think things through. At the moment, any future for our situation seemed impossible.

"Hello?"

All three of us turned around at once, thrilled to hear another voice. A short, portly man stood at the window waving at us, so Cameron went over and opened the window.

"Hi there. I'm the manager of Lakeview Resort, and I wanted to extend our deepest regrets for what's happened to you today."

Hugh raced over to the window in a flash, his face clouded with anger. "Why is the patio door sealed shut?" he demanded.

"At the very least we should be able to open these windows wider if the doors don't work."

The manager clearly didn't expect to be questioned like that, and he stammered for a while before answering. "I... I don't know anything about that, sir."

"Under town by-laws, as manager you are responsible for the safety of your guests. Not the company—you personally. And if there'd been a fire in here, we would have been completely trapped, all because of your negligence. Muriel here was terrified."

He gestured toward me, and the bewildered manager looked over in my direction.

I bristled at being described as terrified as if I were some damsel in distress. If anything, Cameron had been more afraid than me, but I figured there was no point in trying to stop Hugh once he was on a roll.

"I'm so sorry, sir. And madam. And... sir." The manager nodded at Cameron. "I honestly didn't know the doors were sealed; I'll have it attended to as soon as we get you free."

"Fine, but I'll be checking up on you," Hugh said, and he meant it.

I could see why the man got up people's noses, but I also understood the reason he was so annoyed; as beautiful as it was in the bungalow, it clearly wasn't safe.

"Um, yes. Well, in the meantime, here's a package of fresh-baked goodies for breakfast and some bits and pieces to have for your lunch. Let's hope we have you out before dinner time." He held up a bag, which presumably contained breakfast.

"Yes, let's," Hugh replied dryly.

The man scurried away, and Hugh's frown immediately turned into a bright smile as he eyed the contents of the bag. "Ooh, an apple Danish, perfect."

We each grabbed something sweet to eat and settled down on the couches. As we chatted, I loosened up a bit, making sure to stay away from any topic that risked leading us to talk about what happened the night before. We stuck to stories from our school days, and we passed a pleasant couple of hours that way until a familiar face appeared at the window.

"Jasmine!" I ran over to open the window for my friend.

"Hey. I heard you were trapped; I'll be honest, I imagined something more dramatic than being stuck in a cute bungalow..." Jasmine then lowered her voice to a whisper and added, "...with a pair of hotties."

"Shhh." I couldn't help but laugh at my ever-unsubtle friend.

Once she'd arrived, I really wanted to tell Jas what had happened. I needed advice, and for all her faults, Jasmine was the go-to girl for relationship problem-solving. I swear she could have gotten Jennifer Aniston and Brad Pitt back together, if only they'd had the sense to come to her.

She was truly the best. But I couldn't easily lean out, not with the screen in place, and of course, I didn't want Cameron and Hugh to hear what I had to say. I tried to get the message across to Jasmine through a series of facial expressions and small hand gestures, but she just narrowed her eyes with confusion.

"What are you doing? Is this some sort of dance you've made up? Have you got cabin fever already? Watch out, y'all; she's cracking up."

I blushed scarlet as Jasmine shouted across at the guys, but they were deep into one of their friendly debates and barely paid us any attention.

"Look, I'll tell you later," I hissed at her, and her eyes widened.

"Oh, so that was code for something secret? Well, it was terrible. You'll never be a spy, Muriel. You're going to have to tell me—properly—later; I've got to go and see my mom now."

"That'll be nice."

I received a scowl in return. "You have met my mother, haven't you?"

"Yes, I have." I remembered the last time I encountered the senior Ms. Bailey. "Perhaps nice is a strong word. But I'm sure you'll survive."

My enthusiastic thumbs up received a middle finger in reply.

Jasmine promised to stop by later, and just seeing her had calmed me down.

The French press called to me, so I headed toward the kitchen, but as I passed the two guys, Cameron pulled me down between them on the sofa.

"We need to talk," he said, seriously.

I always assumed that the phrase '*we need to talk*' only sounded scary in the context of break-ups, but we weren't even together, and the words made me want to run a mile. Still, I figured I owed them an explanation for my daytime behavior being in stark contrast to the way I acted the night before. But I wasn't sure I had an explanation, and didn't have the time or space to figure it out, so I'd just have to roll with it.

"About last night. Did you enjoy yourself?" The sincerity in Hugh's voice hurt my heart. Why would he ask? How could they think for a second that I didn't enjoy what we shared?

I swallowed hard. "It was the best night of my life. Seriously, it was incredible."

"Great. Ours too," Cameron said brightly. "I can speak for Hugh on that fact."

But Hugh held up his hand. "And there's a 'but' coming." He was astute, as usual.

"There is. Last night was amazing, but—" What was I going to say? "It has to be a one off. It's not going to work. It can't work. It was a terrible, wonderful mistake that can never happen again." Well, that was definitive; on auto-pilot, it seemed I opted for the 'rip off the Band-Aid' approach to sharing bad news.

"But—" Cameron's stunned expression said enough as began to argue. I put my hand on his knee to stop him.

"I have a life in LA. I have a career that's over two thousand miles away from here. I... I find the whole idea of living as a threesome weird, and my parents would never accept us. I'm sorry, but I can't see a future here at all, so it's best we end things now before they've begun."

"Oh," Cameron said, and all three of us fell silent.

I stared at my book without reading it. How might I have avoided getting into such an awkward situation? Perhaps if I'd used my brain instead of my... well, the opposite end of my body I'd have saved us from all the morning after issues.

"Excuse me." I grabbed my book and headed into my bedroom, shutting the door behind me. I needed privacy, partly because I didn't want to hear any bright ideas they might have about how to make this work, but also because I was on the verge of tears, and Muriel Tennyson cried for no man. Or men. Even perfect men. Nobody. Ever.

I angrily swiped a tear from my cheek and lay on top of my bed. That rescue vehicle couldn't get here soon enough.

Chapter Eight
Cameron Moore

Hugh pulled me back onto the couch when I tried to follow Muriel out of the living room.

"We need to talk to her," I insisted.

"She needs space," he replied calmly. "She's already trapped in here with us, and she probably has complicated feelings about last night. Forcing her to talk to us about it isn't going to help our case."

I sighed bitterly, knowing he was right. "The three of us could be happy together. It's so frustrating that she can't see it."

"She isn't blind. She can see it, but doesn't want to admit it. She wants us. If she didn't, she'd have brushed off last night as just a bit of fun." Hugh's rare glimmer of optimism almost shocked me out of my bad mood. "But she wants other things too, things that we can't give her. Bright lights, big city, a glamorous career; that kind of thing."

"That's shallow stuff. Muriel isn't going to let her job rule her life, surely?"

He shrugged. "I wouldn't have thought so, but she needs to reach her own conclusions. Let's give her some space and see what happens."

"Fine."

Even I was aware that I suddenly sounded like a spoiled child. Everything I ever wanted was so tantalizingly close to being mine; she *had* been mine, actually, for a blissful but all-too-short time.

Hugh always ragged on me for being perpetually too sunny, but my outlook saw me through hard times. If you focus on positive thoughts, you get positive results. If that makes me sound like a hippy, then so be it. But right then, I struggled to accept leaving life to chance when it came to Muriel.

It was starting to seem like getting what you want and then losing it was so much worse than never having it, because you understood exactly what you were going to miss out on. What's that old cliche? Better to have loved and lost than never to have loved at all? Bullshit.

I gave myself a mental slap and pulled my mental socks up. No good would come from falling down a rabbit hole of Hugh-like pessimism.

I lifted my head up from the pillow I'd dramatically made with my arms and clicked my fingers in the air. "How about we figure out a nice lunch from the stuff that guy brought in the basket? She can take it to her room if she wants, but it'll be presented by us, with love."

Hugh wrinkled up his nose. "I mean, it's a bit sappy," he complained. "But she'll probably like it, so fine."

All it took was one good idea to brush away my lousy mood. We emptied the basket and found the plastic boxes contained a variety of fresh and vibrant salads: potato, pasta, beets and walnut salad, tuna with corn, coleslaw, and so on. Even though we wouldn't be serving anything worthy of a Michelin-starred restaurant, and we hadn't chopped it with our own bare hands, I hoped she'd appreciate the gesture as we worked on laying out an appetizing spread.

We laid out a tablecloth we'd found in the back of a kitchen cupboard and placed the fine bone chinaware and silver cutlery on top. Given the circumstances, it made a great presentation, even though the salads had to remain in their plastic containers on the table.

I'd pressured Muriel enough for the day, so I let Hugh go and knock on her bedroom door. He called out that we'd made her lunch and she was under no obligation to talk to us if she didn't want to, but she should eat something.

Eventually, her feet padded to the door and then into the hallway with Hugh.

"Ta-da," I said as she entered the room.

Her face lit up like a kid at Christmas. "Oh my god, this looks incredible." She happily took a seat at the table. "Was this all in that package from the guy this morning?"

"Yeah. Looks good, huh? We wanted to make the effort since you're under a lot of stress right now."

"Well, that's really thoughtful," Muriel said, and my heart swelled at her approval.

"Don't be shy, now. Dig in," Hugh said and passed one of only two serving spoons to her.

"Everything, every ingredient we put in for maximum nutrition and to boost energy levels." I winked.

Muriel laughed, took the spoon, and cast her eye over the offerings. "It all looks good; who'd guess emergency rations in a storm would be as great as this?"

"If this looks good, wait and see what we've got you for dessert."

I did *not* intend to sound so suggestive. We hadn't placed the pecan pie out on display, so she took my comment for innuendo and eyed me suspiciously before reaching out to pick a plump grape, which she held aloft. "Are you getting fruity?" she asked and then giggled.

Hugh chuckled and then forked a mound of potato salad into his mouth.

"Aw, I do appreciate the effort y'all have gone to here. And look, it was unfair of me to storm off earlier. I'm just—my head is swirling with a million thoughts right now."

"We understand," Hugh said, and I nodded in agreement. "This is a weird situation for all of us, but even stranger for you being back in your hometown for the first time in years. Have you missed it?"

Muriel gratefully seized the opportunity to talk about something other than our relationship, and we chatted easily for a while about California versus Georgia. I couldn't see the appeal of California compared to our home state. We had everything here, from beautiful beaches to great sports teams and even a thriving movie industry, and everything cost about ten percent of what it would cost out west.

"So yeah, most nights it's just me and my cat Claws, sitting around watching TV, the same thing people do all over the world, I guess."

She explained how life in LA wasn't anywhere near as glamorous as we'd assumed. "Sometimes I'll get together with Poppy, if she isn't away modeling somewhere, or Jasmine if she isn't busy with a new commission, but that's about it, really."

"No guys, then?" Hugh asked.

If I'd asked that exact same thing, Muriel would have climbed out the window for sure, but Hugh had that journalist's knack of asking a question in just the right tone so it sounded casual and encouraged her to answer.

"There have been guys," she began to explain, and a flare of jealousy ran up my spine. "But not many, and it's never lasted long. Like I said yesterday, nobody compares to you two. And no one presents a cold lunch with quite your flare either."

"We worked with what we were given," I said modestly, but my heart soared to hear that she had been pining for us as we had for her. I still didn't understand why she was so determined to live in LA, or to live a lie where she pretended she didn't want to live as a throuple, but it was comforting to find out that at least she cared about us. I began clearing the plates away and sealing the lids on the leftovers, ready to place them in the fridge that had no electricity.

"Well, if you ever change your mind about the whole California career girl thing, you know where we are," I said, and I meant it. I spoke for Hugh too. Both of us would wait a lifetime for her if that was what we needed to do.

"You'll be my first visit, but in the meantime—"

Hugh was busy testing his phone. It still didn't connect. And I busied myself with tidying up, so it took a polite little cough from Muriel to make us turn and really see her. When I did, I almost dropped the pile of plates, and Hugh did drop his phone on the hardwood floor. He didn't even bother to check whether it had smashed.

Muriel was mid way through lifting up her thin white nightgown, which she still wore despite the time of day. She had nothing underneath. She somehow looked even more stunning through my sober eyes than she did last night.

As she tossed away the nightgown and stood proudly naked in front of us, I took in every inch of her pale skin, from her knees to her thighs and from her soft stomach to her perfect breasts with pink, pebbled nipples. She'd had me convinced I would never see her naked again, yet here we were.

"We might not have a future, but we've got the present, so why not have some fun with it?"

Well, what choice did we gentlemen have but to oblige?

Chapter Nine
Muriel Tennyson

What the hell are you doing, Muriel?

A nagging, annoyingly sensible voice in the back of my head reminded me that I'd already decided this must not happen again. It wasn't fair for any of us to have a repeat performance of the exhilarating high and inevitable low that had to follow.

My counter-argument was that while literally stuck in a strange situation, we might as well enjoy ourselves; it lacked logic as much as it was tempting, so temptation won out.

I stood before them, naked and tingling with anticipation.

That same voice of reason pointed out that it was broad daylight, the calm after the storm, and someone could easily peer through the window and see me, but I didn't care at that moment. I only wanted my guys, and from the way they ogled me, they wanted me too.

"Are... are you sure?" Hugh stuttered.

Honestly, the only man who could have a woman strip down in front of him and still wonder whether she was interested.

"Of course I'm sure. Now get over here and kiss me."

He didn't need any more encouragement. Hugh strode across the kitchen and grabbed the back of my head with such lustful ferocity that I lost my breath.

Our lips crushed together, and we kissed; a long, deep, somehow soulful kiss that made any thoughts of the real world disappear. He explored my exposed body with his hands, and as he teasingly brushed past my oh-so-sensitive clit, the sensation almost made me bite his tongue.

Before last night I didn't think it was physically possible to be brought to the very edge of climax in twenty seconds flat, but it turned out you just need the right man. Or men.

"Let's all go to the bedroom," I said, looking over Hugh's shoulder at Cameron. He clearly enjoyed watching me with his best friend. Cam's eyes were heavy with lust and his expression dreamy, but the prospect of joining in had him racing to the bedroom in a flash.

"There's no hurry." Hugh took my hand, and we followed Cameron through the bungalow. "We're going to be here a while, remember?"

"You try telling *this* there's no hurry." Cameron had already removed his robe by the time we reached the bedroom, and he pointed dramatically at his enormous erection.

I licked my lips and smiled.

"On the bed," I commanded, brimming with incredible confidence all of a sudden.

"Yes, boss," Cameron replied as he climbed onto the bed and lay on his back.

I crawled toward him, and we kissed tenderly at first, but as desire overwhelmed us, our greedy tongues began to lick and suck, and his cock bounced against my thigh as I straddled him.

Much as kissing Cam was incredible, I experienced a gnawing sense of something missing.

It seemed they'd broken me and the touch of one man would never again be enough for my body.

Supporting myself on my elbows, I wiggled my ass at Hugh invitingly, and I grinned at the swishing sound of his robe as it instantly fell to the floor.

In a moment, the mattress dipped, and I cried out as Hugh's tongue parted my lips without warning.

He pressed his face into my most intimate area. His tongue danced around my sensitive folds and swept across my little pink pearl, making me shudder in ecstasy.

Cameron pinched my nipples, and that was enough to push me over. Heat and pleasure exploded deep in my core. While they rocked my world, I called out both of their names over and over until my orgasm receded, leaving me deeply, intensely satisfied.

"Your 'O' face is fucking beautiful." Cameron smiled up at me and tucked a stray curl behind my ear.

I'd always been self-conscious about what I looked like when I came. I wondered whether I might pass for a crazy woman on the verge of a demonic sneeze, so he really couldn't have given me a better compliment.

Hugh sat up and gave my ass a light spank, making me yelp as a little thrill ran through me.

But I wanted more. Needed more. I pulled myself up fully onto my hands and knees. "Kneel, Cameron," I said firmly.

"I've gotta say, I like this demanding version of Muriel," he replied while doing exactly as I asked. He kneeled in front of me with his cock a mere inch from my face. I nudged it playfully with my nose, then started licking the sensitive underside, making him moan and whine.

The quiet sound of tearing only just reached my ears, and then Hugh returned, this time with his cock teasing my entrance.

My body automatically pressed back against it, desperate to finally have my brooding man breach and fill me. He eventually relented and took hold of my hips as he entered.

As he deepened his thrust, I took Cameron further into my mouth, until I was stuffed full of both of them; like I was no longer a good girl but some different, uninhibited other version of me.

Hugh started to move, setting a languid rhythm that I replicated on Cameron, so we all moved in sync. For the first time in my life, I felt complete, whole, and like three of us connected in this way was the most natural thing in the world.

"I'm going to come," Cameron warned after a few minutes; my blowjob skills were apparently much better than I realized. Or else the whole erotic threesome blew him away as much as it did me.

He let go of my hair to allow me to take a breath, but I just carried on sucking him. I was equally turned on and excited about tasting him.

Hot, salty cum sprayed into my mouth while I gazed up at him through my lashes. I watched the happiest man on earth in the throes of ecstasy while I sucked and swallowed every last drop of his seed.

For a minute or two, I licked his delicious cock up and down, enjoying every last drop of what he had to give me until his dick had completely softened and dropped from my mouth.

"I have an idea," I said, and Hugh paused his thrusting to hear me out. "Hugh, lie on the bed here."

"Sure." He reluctantly pulled out of me and lay down.

I turned to face away from him and then straddled his muscular thighs.

"Oh, God," he moaned, on realizing what I had planned for him. "This is a dream come true."

I slid onto his cock and set my own slow rhythm, bouncing up and down with long strokes, knowing full well that Hugh would admire the curve of my ass from that angle.

"Oh God, that's amazing. You're amazing."

Cameron appeared in front of me and started playing with my body, pinching my nipples and rubbing my clit until I almost blacked out from the intensity of the different sensations.

It was hard to keep grinding on Hugh when I was so distracted, but I kept up my rhythm, determined to please him as much as it also pleased me.

I leaned forward to hold on to his thighs for extra support and to give him an even better viewing angle; the small whimper that escaped his lips told me I'd succeeded.

My toes curled as I trembled on top of Hugh. His cock hit the perfect spot at the exact same time as Cameron gently flicked my clit.

I screamed, and it seemed like my voice came from a whole different person, wild and completely unabashed.

The sight and sound of my climax must have been too much for Hugh, because he grabbed my hips in response and began thrusting up, growling aggressively. As he plunged into me for the final time, he emitted a guttural moan and held me still on his twitching cock until he was completely spent.

"Holy shit," he said finally as I climbed off him, and the three of us settled under the covers.

"Holy shit indeed," I agreed.

"How did you guess that reverse cowgirl is his favorite thing in the whole world?" Cameron asked. "And I do mean favorite thing, not just favorite position. I'd say you'd choose it over winning ten million dollars, wouldn't you, Hugh?"

"Yup," Hugh replied lazily, "no contest."

I merely shrugged. "Hugh's a guy, and you all appreciate having an ass in your face."

Both guys laughed at that, but I wasn't joking.

"Fair," Cameron replied. "Anyway, that was incredible."

We three clasped hands and lay together in a happy, drowsy silence for a while.

I knew then I'd never get anywhere close to such bliss with anybody else except those two men. How would I ever go back to normal life once I'd discovered they could make me feel *that* way?

Or have a normal boyfriend?

It was impossible to imagine being satisfied with one man after discovering four hands were way better than two.

I didn't want to share my confused thoughts with the guys in case I got their hopes up, so I decided to tell them about a much less important problem. "I'm hungry. Was there anything else in that basket?"

Cameron laughed. "There are plenty of leftovers, but there's also a dessert waiting for us."

We all shrugged on our robes and padded through the bungalow.

Cameron headed straight toward the countertop. "A rich pecan pie is exactly what we need." And a few minutes later we ate the sweet dessert from plates on our laps.

Cam sat at the bottom of the couch, and when we'd finished eating, he placed our plates on the floor and raised my feet to place them in his lap. He massaged my heels, toes, and the balls of my feet. Effortlessly, he soothed the aches and pains I'd developed thanks to wearing a brand-new pair of heels at the rehearsal dinner the night before.

Happy, sleepy, and content, I closed my eyes.

"Would you like me to read your book to you?" Hugh asked, pulling up a chair beside me, holding *Emma* in his hands. "Or is that too cheesy?"

"Oh, it's cheesy, but yes please, I'd love it."

He began to read. His dulcet tones made him a perfect narrator.

Leaning back and dropping grapes into my mouth, I felt like a pampered Greek goddess. I pondered the fact that this could be my real life, if only I was brave enough to seize it. Would anyone really care if I was in a three-way relationship? And if they did, would I care that they cared? At that moment, it seemed as long as I had these two men to love and to love me back, I didn't need anything or anyone else.

Hugh reached the end of a chapter and paused. "Are you actually listening?" he asked in a mock-accusatory tone.

"Guilty as charged. I'm just enjoying your voice. Say, when you two have been in relationships together before, how have people treated you?"

Cameron stopped rubbing my feet to give his full attention to the conversation. "Okay, for the most part. Nothing's ever lasted long enough for us to make a big announcement about it, but we've been seen around town with one woman before, and nobody seemed to mind."

"Except Elijah," Hugh corrected him.

Cameron rolled his eyes and groaned.

"Elijah from school?" I asked, and both guys nodded.

"He saw both of us kiss a girl in a restaurant one time, and he came over and told us we would all burn in Hell for eternity," Cam said.

"For *all* eternity," Hugh corrected. "And he made a bit of a scene, so we had to leave, and it really upset the girl."

"What a dick," I said.

It didn't surprise me. Elijah was the biggest snitch in school and a total pain in the ass. Once he noticed me doing my English homework in math class, and he told both the English and math teachers about it; I got a week's detention. One of my biggest regrets in life was not punching him in the nose when I had a chance.

"Yep, he's a dick, all right," Hugh agreed. "He's a councilman now, too, so I have run-ins with him all the time. But other than that, it's not been a big deal. Why do you ask?"

"Oh, just wondering." I still didn't want to admit I was considering how we might make the trio last longer than a day, but I had to confide in someone, and right then, there was nobody else available. "Do you honestly believe it could work—the three of us together, I mean?"

"Of course, it could work," Cameron said, slapping my thigh excitedly.

Hugh looked less convinced, so I waited for his response with bated breath.

"From our perspective, there wouldn't be any problems," he answered carefully. "We've already said we want nothing more than to be with you. But you have to be certain it's what you want, and I don't know if you are."

I frowned. "I think I'm certain."

"*Thinking* you're certain isn't the same as *being* certain," Hugh pointed out, and in my head, I cursed him for being so damn clever.

Cameron's eyes narrowed like he was mad at his best friend, but Hugh was undeterred. "Less than an hour ago you specifically said that we didn't have a future; so, what's changed?"

"I've changed," I protested. "What we did in there, and this," I gestured at my feet and the book that Hugh still held. "This has changed my mind. I think we can do it. It'll be difficult with me living so far away at the moment, but this is what I want my life to be like, so I'm absolutely willing to try."

"Fantastic!" Cameron exclaimed, stopping Hugh from saying anything more. "I knew you'd see sense, Muriel."

I nodded, smiling, but before I replied, the sound of another massive crash made us all jump in alarm. We all jumped up and ran to the windows. The massive tree that had us trapped jerking about as if it had come to life. A tapping sound at another window made us turn to see Poppy waving in.

"Oh my god, Poppy!" I ran over to the window and opened it as wide as it would go.

"Hey, baby girl. I called in a favor and got Cooper and Nolan to come down with their truck and a winch... look, you're free."

With mixed feelings, I watched the tree being dragged away from the door, and Cameron pulled it open with a flourish.

"Freedom," he yelled dramatically as Cooper and Nolan approached the doorway. "Come on in, bold rescuers. Welcome to our little prison."

They all came inside, and nerves overshadowed my happiness at being free as they looked between the three of us with varying degrees of amusement evident in their smiles. Poppy was the most blatant, with a single eyebrow fully raised.

I was suddenly very conscious that we were all wearing nothing other than robes in the afternoon. I excused myself and headed back to the bedroom to get changed.

As I rummaged through my suitcase for a comfortable outfit, I felt like slapping myself. The rescuers brought with them a reality check.

It was all very well talking about a three-way relationship when we were the only three people in the world, but the way my friend and those men had looked at us made my blood run cold. I didn't want to admit anything to them. I felt ashamed and fearful of their reaction, and I was also ashamed of how I felt. It was so confusing.

And our rescuers were all nice, kind people.

What if we bumped into someone like Elijah or my mother? My stomach churned at the prospect of telling people or of anyone finding out about what had happened: what was happening.

I might be about to let my guys down at the first possible hurdle.

I pulled on my casual clothes, a pleated tartan skirt and a sweater, and put my hair into a high ponytail. The bedroom smelled of sex, so I carefully secured the door shut when I went back out into the living room.

"Where's Cameron?" I asked, noticing he'd disappeared.

"He's gone to see Vic; reckons he'll need some help with the clean up," Hugh explained. That was Cameron, always ready to jump in and help out. My heart swelled, but guilt tempered my pride as I remembered how excited he'd been to hear I wanted to try a relationship with them both.

That was rash, Muriel.

Hugh looked at me carefully, probably sensing that I had a lot on my mind, but I brushed him off with a breezy smile.

"I'll go and get dressed then, I guess," he said.

As soon as he left the room, I turned to Poppy, determined to distract her before she asked me anything about Hugh and Cameron. "What happened to you during the storm?" I asked. "How did you end up with Cooper and Nolan?"

Poppy hesitated, seemingly wanting to tell me something, but stopped herself. "I'll tell you later. I'm helping them with the rescues, but I suspect we've both got a *lot* to talk about."

She waggled her perfectly manicured brows, and my cheeks flushed scarlet. "I've no idea what you're talking about," I protested.

She rolled her eyes. "Uh huh, I'm sure. See ya later."

As I watched her leave with the two good-looking men, an even more handsome man placed his hands on my shoulders. He started massaging them, and I leaned into it, sighing happily.

"You okay?"

"Yes," I lied. "Just tired, that's all. Say, do you need a ride home? I doubt you'll get a cab anytime soon, and my rental arrived before the storm got going last night."

"That'd be good, but do you mind dropping me off at my folks' place? I'd better check up on them; my mom can be... challenging when she's stressed."

I'd met Hugh's mom a few times, so I knew he was being polite. She was a total battle-axe and fiercely protective of her only son.

I'd probably admire her if she didn't happen to hate me. I wasn't being paranoid; she made her feelings very clear every time Cameron and I went over to do homework at her house.

If she ever found out her son was in a three-way relationship with Cameron and me. I'd probably have to leave the country or risk finding a horse's head in my bed.

"That's fine, but I'd better drop you off at the door and then flee."

He shook his head, laughing.

"I don't know why you think my mom doesn't like you. She acts the same with everyone. It's the way she is."

"She was never rude to Cameron."

"Well, that's different. Voldemort himself would be charmed by Cameron; it's those freckles and that ridiculous enthusiasm of his."

He wasn't wrong, but I was still certain I'd be better off avoiding Hugh's mother, at least while my guilt about what we'd done together was still fresh. Knowing my social awkwardness, I'd probably end up telling her all about our night. And I'd end up murdered on the spot.

We tidied up the apartment a bit, figuring that the cleaners would have enough to deal with for the next few days, then I grabbed my keys, and we set out.

Chapter Ten
Hugh Davis

Muriel was quiet as we set out for my parent's house. Worryingly quiet.

I shouldn't have let her say that she wanted to make things work between us. I'm sure she meant every word at the time, but you can't count on things said under the influence of the post-coital glow.

The way her eyes widened when we told her about our run-in with Elijah made it obvious that she wasn't ready for that sort of stick or for people finding out about our throuple.

"When do you head home?" I asked, breaking the silence.

"I *am* home," Muriel said with a beaming smile. "But if you mean LA, my flight is in a couple of days. I promised my parents I'd hang out with them after the wedding, so I extended my trip a little."

"Cool." I tried to hide my disappointment that she planned on leaving so soon.

The roads were pretty rough after the storm, and all kinds of debris and flooded sections made progress slow. Behind the wheel, Muriel navigated the obstacles like a rally driver, and I couldn't help giving her the occasional glance of admiration. I do like a practical woman.

"Mind if I put some music on?" I asked.

When we all hung out after school, we loved listening to music, and often ended up arguing about it. Cameron was into country, which in my not-very-humble opinion isn't *real* music, while Muriel and I both liked The Smiths, The Cure, and Depeche Mode. My tastes had barely changed in the last five years, and unfortunately, neither had Cameron's, so I was willing to bet Muriel would still like the same bands too.

She gestured for me to go ahead without taking her eyes off the road.

I leaned over and switched on her car stereo. Her phone beeped, the Bluetooth automatically connecting to her fancy rental car, and to my horrified delight, Cher's version of The Shoop Shoop Song began to blare from the speakers.

"Oh my God, switch it off," Muriel screeched, her cheeks instantly flushing with understandable embarrassment.

"Watch that trash can!" I called out, bringing her attention back to the treacherous road while I tried and failed to stop myself from laughing at her.

"I don't normally listen to this stuff. It... it was Jasmine's playlist," Muriel protested, but I was not stupid.

"And why would she use your phone for her own playlist?" I asked.

She groaned in defeat. "All right, Mr. Investigative Journalist, enough of the third degree. I like stupid classic pop music, okay?"

I patted her on the shoulder. "You're in a safe space here, Muriel; your secret's safe with me. Although, this does make me wonder whether you ever really did like The Smiths."

We'd once spent a magical time together in my parents' yard and I'd played her their songs on my guitar for a whole evening.

"Remember that night Cameron didn't hang out with us, and you made me listen to you play a whole album on your guitar?" Her tone suggested it was a painful memory.

"I *made* you listen?"

"Well, yeah. You didn't really believe I enjoyed it, did you? I pretended to like those cool bands to impress you." She glanced over at me and caught a flash of hurt on my face. "I mean, I did enjoy that night because I like your voice so much? Yes. I loved listening to you and you were so hot just strumming that guitar. It was only the tunes that I didn't like. And the lyrics, if I'm honest."

"Oh, that's all?" The compliments softened the blow of finding out that I'm the only one of our trio who has good musical taste.

I started dancing along to the stupid song. "I have to admit though, this is pretty catchy." My attempt to twerk while seated and without fully knowing what twerking involved soon had Muriel struggling to keep her composure.

"Yeah, Hugh, move those hips." She laughed. "It's like watching Mr. Darcy at a rave."

"You can't handle my moves," I joked.

The song finally came to an end, but something equally awful started playing next, so I picked up her phone to find something decent. I noticed her lock screen wallpaper was a picture of her, Jasmine, and Poppy at what looked like a pool party.

Muriel looked incredible, of course. She wore a white bikini top with a pleated skirt, and her hair was piled casually on top of her head. She had her arms wrapped around her friends, and they were all pulling stereotypical 'influencer' faces, although I suspected their tongues were firmly placed in their cheeks for this photo.

Muriel fitted in there. She belonged there, surrounded by beautiful, glamorous people and a swimming pool with a glorious view of the big city. I glanced out the window. Even at its best, we couldn't offer the lifestyle she'd become used to, and after the storm, it would take a while for things to be back to their best.

"Are you snooping?" Muriel asked.

I guiltily put the phone down, letting the nightmare playlist rumble on.

"No, of course not. I just noticed your lock screen, that's all. It's a lovely photo."

"Thanks, that was somebody's birthday party. Couldn't tell you who, though. That's the problem with LA; it's all so impersonal. You just go places to be seen; it's all insincere, you know?"

"It sounds like hell."

"For you, it would be. For me, it's been kind of fun, but lately I've wondered whether there's more to life than parties and cute clothes."

"There definitely is."

We turned off the main road onto a narrower one that was only used by farmers and locals who were in the know about shortcuts. She apparently hadn't forgotten where she was from, even if she was a bit shaky with a few old school friends' names.

"So, you think I should move back here for good?"

"Er..." I stuttered as I tried to process the question. Was she seriously considering moving back, or was this just small talk? And if she did mean it, how should I answer?

Of course, she should move back; because I was selfish, and I wanted nothing more than to see her every day for the rest of her life. But that didn't make it the right decision for her.

Cameron and I would do everything in our power to make her happy, but how would we offer more than what she had in LA, and what I saw in that photo?

"Shit, look over there." Just down the road a little way, I spotted a large vehicle that seemed to have been struck by a falling tree. The back windshield was clearly shattered. The route was so quiet that anyone trapped inside might be stuck there for hours.

Muriel pulled up behind the Volvo and leaped out of the car.

I joined her, and we peered through the windows to see an old lady at the wheel, unconscious.

"Damn it."

I tried the door, but it was locked, so I knocked desperately at the window. It took a worrying minute before she stirred, and Muriel and I heaved huge sighs of relief before the woman looked at us with stern eyes.

"What are you doing?" she demanded, as though we'd wandered into her home uninvited.

I shouted through the closed window, explaining that we'd been passing by, and she appeared to be in trouble. After a little coaxing, she agreed to unlock the door.

"I think she's in shock," I murmured to Muriel, who nodded in agreement. "We should take her to the hospital."

"Ma'am, I'm Muriel. What's your name?"

"Agnes. Agnes Butterfield."

"That's a beautiful name." Cameron wasn't the only charmer in town; I could turn it on if I needed to. "Now, Agnes, let's get you checked out at the hospital. Do you want to take my arm?"

The lady's face transformed from stern to bashful as I reached down to offer the use of my elbow as support.

"That's quite an offer, young man," Agnes said. "But perhaps you should take me dancing instead?"

Muriel laughed, and I had to grin too.

"We'll see about the dancing once we've got you a full bill of health. You must have had a nasty shock when that tree fell."

"Pah, it was nothing. I just had a little nap to pass the time. But if you insist, we'll go to the hospital on the way to the dance."

Muriel climbed back into the driver's seat while I got Agnes settled in the back. Once back in the passenger seat, I tested my phone for a GPS signal.

"I'm still getting nothing on my phone. Do you know the way?"

"Yep. Honestly, I know these roads like the back of my hand," Muriel replied as she pulled away.

Agnes chatted happily all the way to the hospital, with only the occasional strange comment that suggested she might be suffering from shock, heat stroke, or a concussion.

"So, are you two an item?" she called out from the back seat, and I looked at Muriel awkwardly.

"I'll let you take that one," I said, and Muriel glanced in the rearview mirror with a warm smile.

"We're... it's complicated."

My heart sank a little. I'd hoped for a simple affirmation.

Muriel gave out very mixed signals and I had no clue what to make of them. One minute she casually talked about moving back here, and the next she couldn't even tell a stranger that I was her boyfriend.

I wished I could interview Muriel properly, pull out my pad and pen and bombard her with questions, but I knew from her behavior this morning that if I pushed too hard, she'd run.

Agnes seemed to understand what Muriel meant, and she tapped the side of her nose conspiratorially. "Complicated, I see. Your secret's safe with me."

Muriel started giggling, and I had to nudge her in the ribs to stop her.

"What does she think I meant?" she whispered.

"That we're having an affair, probably," I whispered back, and Agnes piped up again to confirm my suspicions.

"I had a lot of '*complications*' with young men back in my day until I met my Richard, and then everything became perfectly simple. Fifty-three years, we were married. I never even looked at another man after I met him."

"That's really beautiful." A sorrowful longing seemed to replace the amusement in Muriel's voice, and her expression was pensive.

"But you kids have fun while you're young," Agnes continued. "You spend a long time dead."

"Very good point," I replied, knowing full well that I needed to be poked with a cattle prod before I'd allow myself to *just* have fun. I never would be a *just* have fun type of person.

Except when Muriel was around.

And especially when we were naked together.

Only then did cold, harsh reality disappear, and I got a taste of the easy-going paradise that Cameron lived in full-time.

We got Agnes to the hospital, and I promised that I'd interview her for a story about her ordeal once she had fully recovered. Apparently, it would give her extra 'street cred' in her residential home. Muriel offered to do her makeup for the essential flattering photo and teach me about filters. Normally I preferred raw, untouched images, but I had an inkling that Agnes would enjoy a little soft focus.

Eventually, we pulled up outside my parents' home. It wasn't much, a simple whitewashed Craftsman-style cottage, but my granddad built it himself, and I hoped it would always stay in the family.

"I'll give you a call soon," Muriel said. "Once the signal's working again, anyway."

But I really didn't want her to go. Even though we'd spent almost twenty-four hours in pretty much constant company, I wanted her to stay. And I wanted Cameron with us too; as much as I loved spending time with Muriel, the idea of being in a couple with her wasn't right—the three of us were more than the sum of our parts—we balanced each other out.

"Aw, come in and say hi to my parents. Mom might be a bit of a character, but she doesn't bite. I'm sure she'd love to see you again. Why not have a quick sweet tea and then go?"

Muriel hesitated. I didn't blame her; even though I had denied it earlier, I knew my mom never liked Muriel, though she never told me why.

She'd never been rude to other girls I'd brought home, not that there had been many, and anyway, Muriel and I had been entirely platonic back then.

But it had been at least five years since they last met, so I figured perhaps my mom had forgotten whatever issue she had. Muriel was a grown woman, and such a great one. Also my mom was awesome, so it made sense that they should get along, and it seemed important that they did.

"If you come in, I promise I'll never make you listen to The Smiths again for the rest of our lives." I couldn't come up with a better bargaining chip on the spot, but that was a big one.

"And you'll dance to Thong Song again for me, but standing up this time?"

"Naked, if you like," I promised.

That made her blush, but it must have tipped the balance because she switched off the ignition with a sigh.

Chapter Eleven
Hugh Davis

We walked up the path toward the house, and before we arrived at the door, my mom had opened it and waited for me with open arms.

"Mom." I wrapped her in a hug; I wasn't too proud to admit that I was a momma's boy, even if it didn't fit the brooding stereotype.

"We've been so worried. Cameron's dad called and told us you were trapped. What the heck happened?"

"How about we tell you over some tea?" I gestured toward Muriel, who stood awkwardly at the bottom of the steps. "Remember Muriel?"

Mom's eyes immediately narrowed. "Yes."

"Well, she was trapped too, so she deserves some of your amazing sweet tea, don't you think?"

There followed a long silence that made me cringe before my mom finally relented. "If you say so. Come in, take your shoes off."

Mom walked inside, and I gave Muriel an apologetic gesture as she walked up the steps looking like she wanted to kill me.

We took off our shoes and headed through to the kitchen, where my dad sat watching the local news channel.

"Bad storm last night, Hugh." Dad didn't remove his gaze from the TV.

"He knows that, Hank," Mom snapped. "I told you, he was stuck in some bungalow somewhere. I can't *think* how that happened."

Muriel was admiring an antique sign on the kitchen wall, so she didn't notice the evil eyes directed at the back of her head.

I glared at my mother and hissed, "Be nice."

"Fine," she mouthed back at me, but the way she slammed things around in the kitchen as she prepared the refreshments told me everything I needed to know.

What made me think bringing Muriel home would be a good idea?

If I was honest with myself, I hoped if the two women finally hit it off, the idea of moving here might appeal to Muriel even more.

As it was, she was more likely than ever to scurry off on an early flight back to LA and never return.

"There's your tea. I've got ironing to do." Mom left the room without even looking at us.

After gesturing for Muriel to pull up a stool, when she sat down I placed my hand on the small of her back. I was sure she flinched as I touched her.

Perhaps being intimate in my parents' house made her uncomfortable, which was hardly unreasonable given the reception we experienced.

I whispered to her, low so that my dad couldn't hear. "I'm so sorry, that wasn't acceptable at all. I'm going to talk to her."

Leaving Muriel with a glass of sweet tea, my dad, and the TV for company, I headed to the basement where I found my mom and discovered that it is possible to iron with ferocity.

"Mom, what's wrong?"

"Wrong? Nothing, darling. This darn ironing does not do itself and it has been piling up, and—"

I placed my hand on the iron, holding it still before she could grab it and burn another pair of dad's pants.

"Mom. You aren't subtle. What is it about Muriel that gets you so riled up?"

She looked up, and I noticed the dark, doubtful look she gave me was exactly the same as I see in the mirror every day. It freaked me out a little, though I couldn't put a finger on why.

"She's not right for you."

"Right for me?" I scowled and threw my hands in the air in frustration. "We're just friends. We've always been just friends!" I shouted, feeling only slightly guilty.

It wasn't technically a lie; if Muriel can call us '*complicated,*' I can call us friends. And anyway, for the majority of the time my mom had known her, we were exactly that and nothing more.

"I've seen the way you look at her." My mom finally dropped the wrinkled garment she was holding back into the basket and the pretense of ironing. "And I'll never forget the way she used to drool over Cameron. She always liked him, not you. You didn't see it, and I never had the heart to tell you. But it's about time you realize it before you make a fool of yourself and get your heart broken."

I closed my eyes tight and pinched the bridge of my nose. It had been a long day, and the last thing I needed was my mother stating aloud my greatest fear.

"It's not like that, Mom."

"You think I don't know my own son? You're crazy about her. She uses you because you're so close to Cameron. I see the type of girl she is, believe me."

My brain throbbed against my skull.

My mom didn't know about my arrangement with Cameron and our preferences. That was only because Cameron and I had never gotten serious enough with anyone to make it worthwhile telling folks about it. I'd gladly explain everything to my parents if I had a relationship that was going to last more than a couple of months. But if Mom was already sure that Muriel was only using me to get to Cameron, explaining we were a threesome would only deepen her conviction, and she would keep touching that open nerve of mine for the rest of my life.

"Please believe me, you have no idea about our friendship. She's not using me; she would never treat anyone badly. She's a kind, honest and funny person, and you two would hit it off if you just gave her a chance."

"She's no good." Mom shook her head.

She was unmoveable, and I was done.

No matter how much I adored my mom, I wouldn't listen to her bad mouth Muriel. I was too mad to speak, so I just turned and headed back up the stairs, desperate to get out of this place instead of listening to poisoned words.

"Muriel, are you ready to go?"

"We're watching football," she replied.

I walked through the kitchen to find her sitting on the couch with my dad watching someone play someone else. I knew nothing about sports and didn't care to learn none, but seeing Muriel chatting easily to my dad about the game was like a balm for my soul. At least they were able to get along.

Perhaps he could talk Mom around, I thought briefly, before laughing bitterly to myself. Mom was so headstrong, and Dad so chill that he probably couldn't convince her the Pope was Catholic if she set her mind on denying it.

"It's getting kind of late; don't you want to visit your parents?"

She gave me a curious look. "Why? Do you want to come and see them too?"

I shrugged. "Sure. My mom's not in the entertaining mood, and there's only so long I can watch folks running around with a ball before I start wanting to scratch my own eyes out, so I might as well tag along. If you don't mind, of course."

"Not at all." Muriel jumped up from the couch and gave my dad a friendly squeeze on the shoulder. "Bye, Mr. Davis."

"See you soon, Muriel."

As she left the room, Dad gave me a thumbs up that made me smile despite myself.

I didn't bother saying goodbye to my mom, and of course, she didn't come up to wave us off, so we just climbed back into Muriel's car and drove away.

"I like your dad," Muriel said finally. "I can't remember seeing him much when we were kids, but he's a real sweetie."

"Yeah, he's great. He used to work a couple jobs, so I didn't see him much either. He's like the opposite of my mom, isn't he?"

Muriel chuckled and nodded her agreement. "They're opposites, kind of like you and Cam, in a way."

She was joking, but it hit too close to home to be amusing for me.

"Do you think I'm cynical?" I asked, and Muriel gave me a wry side-eye look.

"Um, is that a serious question?"

I bristled slightly. "Of course it is. I want to know."

"Hugh, darlin', in first grade, you tried to convince the whole class to boycott the Tooth Fairy because you figured she was ripping us off."

"Well, to be fair—"

"In second grade, you gave a speech at recess about how Santa is just a tool parents use to get kids to behave."

"Was I wrong?"

"We were seven. And now you're a grown man who chooses to stay in his small town to fight corruption rather than get a cushy big-city job that you deserve. You're the most cynical person I've ever met, and it's what makes you so amazing."

I reached over and touched her thigh; she didn't flinch this time. "Thank you."

She sniffed dismissively. "No need to thank me for telling you the truth. Why do you ask, anyway?"

"I'm starting to suspect I get my pessimistic outlook from my mother."

"No shit. Did she tell you why she doesn't like me, then?"

It was probably best not to tell her. Not least because the reason Mom's words made me so mad was that I'd had the exact same suspicion before. How could one woman like Cameron and me the same amount when we were so different?

And who wouldn't choose Cameron's sunny nature over my surliness and weird obsession with local politics? Muriel had never given any indication she had a preference, but now that my mom had mentioned it, I couldn't get it out of my mind.

"She's fine, she just... she suspects we're secretly dating."

"Why would that make her mad, though? She was spitting feathers about me being in her house just now."

"I—" My mind was blank; I couldn't come up with an excuse, which left only the truth. "She thinks you're using me to get close to Cameron."

Muriel switched off the music. "Oh."

We drove on in silence.

Chapter Twelve
Muriel Tennyson

As we drove along the semi-flooded roads to my parents' home, I silently cursed Poppy's thoughtfulness and her ability to wrap men around her little finger. Why did she have to go and get us rescued? If she hadn't made Cooper and Nolan prioritize me over other resort guests, I'd probably still be happily stuck in an isolated bungalow with my guys.

The three of us had such a great time in the bubble of our little prison, and ironically, I'd never felt so free.

Freedom meant not dealing with parents, jobs, and everything else. I only wanted to drag two men back into bed and let the real world drift away.

I'd always known Hugh's mom didn't like me, but I would never have guessed that she thought I was using her son.

My knuckles turned white as I gripped the steering wheel hard while imagining the piece of my mind I'd give her if Hugh would only let me turn around. She was tough, but she'd never seen a pissed Muriel Tennyson.

"So you don't agree with her?" I asked uncertainly.

Hugh was close to his mom, and he respected her opinion.

"Of course not!" he exclaimed, a little too brightly for my liking. "That's why I wanted to get out of there. Anyway, if we did manage to make something work between the three of us, she'd soon realize she was wrong. She's just protective, that's all. I shouldn't have mentioned it."

"Did you tell her what's really happening between us?"

"Nope."

Even though it was for the best, I couldn't help but feel hurt. Why didn't he want to shout about us from the rooftops? Did he have reservations about the three of us in a relationship?

He clearly sensed my tension, and he was smart enough to understand the reason for it.

"Earlier, you told a total stranger we were complicated. You can't expect me to tell my own mother what's going on when I don't even have any idea what 'complicated' is supposed to mean."

Damn him for always being right. We pulled up to my parents' place, and I turned to him.

His face was tired but all the more handsome for it, all unshaven and disheveled in yesterday's clothes. He looked like a true old-fashioned gumshoe.

I instinctively reached out and placed a light peck on his lips, and his soulful eyes gazed back at me in surprise.

"I said it was complicated because it is, but there has to be a way to make it work, doesn't there?"

He shrugged in reluctant agreement. "If Cameron were here, he'd have us looking at house listings together by now. We'd probably be on our way to buy a dog, too."

"And you'd be quoting statistics about relationships failing within six months of buying a place together, and I'd be telling you both to hush your mouth," I said, laughing. "And yet you don't consider us complicated, right? Come on, let's go see my parents."

I stepped out of the car and walked up to the front door. Taking a deep breath, I knocked but got no answer. I tried again, harder this time; still nothing.

"Perhaps they're out shopping?" Hugh suggested, but I shook my head. They would never have gone out with the roads in such a mess. Not unless they had an emergency. My throat tightened with worry, and I pounded harder and harder, even though the house was clearly empty.

Hugh took a walk around the building, but it all appeared intact—the storm mustn't have hit this area anywhere near as hard.

"What if they're stuck somewhere like Agnes was?" My voice trembled.

Hugh wrapped an arm around me and pulled me close enough to breathe in the comforting scent of his skin.

I couldn't believe I'd spent all weekend dreading seeing my parents, blaming my mom for my reluctance to start a relationship with Hugh and Cameron, when they might be stuck somewhere, injured or worse.

"Hey, do they drive a green station wagon, by any chance?" Hugh asked, looking over my shoulder. I spun my head around to see my dad's car, probably the oldest, most beat-up car in Georgia, driving down the road toward us.

"That's them," I said with relief and ran down to greet them.

As my mom stepped out of the car, I gave her a big squeeze. "Where have you been? I've been worried sick."

Dad joined us on the sidewalk. "That's what we should be asking you, Missy. Your mom's had us out looking for you since you didn't send her a photo of the dinner venue last night like you promised."

Damn, I forgot. Not that a text would have gotten through anyway, but maybe Cameron could have passed on a message for me.

"I'm so sorry, but we've been trapped. A tree collapsed in front of my bungalow in the storm, trapping us in there all day."

"We? We who?" Mom asked. She glanced back at the house with a raised eyebrow and added, "Is that Hugh Davis?"

I gulped.

Hugh was standing on the porch, and he raised a hand to wave at my parents when he noticed them looking over.

"Yeah, he... dropped me off after Chrissy's rehearsal dinner when the storm erupted. He had to sleep on the couch. It wasn't comfortable, but better than nothing." I was over-explaining; I always did when I was lying or felt guilty, but Mom just smiled.

"Let's get you both inside. It sounds like you've had quite a night."

We headed up to the house.

When we reached Hugh, my dad gave him a friendly pat on the shoulder. "Thanks for taking care of my girl."

Hugh shook his head with a smile. "Believe me, she doesn't need any taking care of."

"Ah, she might act tough, but she'd have been glad you were with her."

"Dad, shut up." My cheeks flushed, as I turned into embarrassed teenager mode. That sense of regression only worsened when we entered, and the smell of my parents' home filled my nostrils. It was like freshly baked sugar cookies and plastic toys, and it made me want to head up to my old room, sit on my bed and write in my diary about Cameron and Hugh again.

What would teenage Muriel, that conscientious, guilty, 'good' Southern girl, think about what her older self did with her two friends last night? Her head would probably explode, I figured. Back then, I didn't even know it was possible—or legal—to do half the things we did together.

"Muriel, are you okay?" My focus had wandered far away, and I suddenly found myself sitting at the kitchen counter, with Hugh next to me and my slightly concerned mother on the other side.

I gave my head a shake. "Yes, yes, I'm fine. I'm just happy to be home, is all."

"Well, we do miss you," Dad said as he grabbed us some cookies and Cokes and joined us. "But we're proud of what you're doing over there in California."

Mom nodded. "Oh yes, sweetie. You remember Beth Ramsey, who lived down the road when you were young? Brown hair, dressed kinda like Julia Roberts in *Pretty Woman*?"

"Uh, yeah, sure." In truth I had no idea who Mom was talking about and I wasn't sure I'd seen the movie, but I'd learned that it's always best to go along with moms when they started gossiping about random people.

"She was a dance instructor, wasn't she?" Hugh asked.

My mom rolled her eyes with a smirk. "Yeah, *that's* what she called it. Anyway, Patty next door said that Beth's daughter had said she'd seen you in an ad on her phone, for some high-end sneakers, I think it was?"

"I did a campaign for Shingo, yeah," I replied.

"Well, needless to say, everyone at the club is very jealous that my daughter is famous."

Hugh laughed politely, but I knew he'd be dying inside at the idea that doing ads was something to aspire to. He'd been encouraging about my work at the rehearsal dinner, but I didn't for one minute believe he actually respected it—compared to what he did, I was just a walking billboard.

"I don't know, Mom," I said, chewing on my nail.

She slapped my hand out of my mouth and wagged my finger at me; it was a lifelong nervous habit.

"Don't you consider it a bit shallow, what I do? I wonder if I should be doing something more with my life."

"Like what?" Dad asked.

Three searching sets of eyes focused on me. I didn't have any answer; having studied fashion at college didn't exactly qualify me for much.

For the past few months, I'd had a nagging sense that something was missing in my life, a feeling that intensified over the past twenty-four hours.

Of course, Hugh and Cameron had made me aware of a hole that needed filling but I needed more than just a relationship complete with hot sex.

I craved fulfillment, passion, and satisfaction, and as fun as photoshoots and free cocktails were, they didn't light a fire in me like obscure by-laws excited Hugh or helping people excited Cameron.

Even Jasmine, one of the shallowest people in my friendship circle, had a passion for the elaborate costumes she designed.

Me? I just sold stuff.

With no idea of how to answer the question, I just threw my hands in the air and then took a big bite of cookie.

"You could be an 'influencer' for good causes," Hugh suggested. When I raised an eyebrow, he went on to elaborate. "You can advertise cute shoes, but you can also use your position to help people and raise funds, like to rebuild places around here that the storm has ruined. I dunno, maybe?"

Hugh shrugged dismissively, but if my parents hadn't been here, I'd have kissed him so hard he'd have passed out.

"That's genius. I can do that. And you know what? I'm going to start with Agnes."

My heart swelled even more to see my moody man smile.

"Agnes Butterfield? She is such a lovely woman," Mom said, and she didn't add any gossipy facts about her, which meant the woman must be a saint.

"I'm going to get her a new car." I slammed my hand on the table with determination. "My followers are nice, and they've all got grandmas, so they can relate to the issue. If they can pay two hundred dollars for a pair of sneakers, goddammit they can donate twenty to a lovely old lady."

"Language, Muriel," Mom barked.

I mouthed an apology. I'd almost forgotten where I was, I was so pumped up and inspired.

"It sounds like a wonderful idea," Dad said. "And if you're going to focus on local issues, perhaps we'll see you around here more often?"

"You might. Say, will Cameron like this idea?" I addressed the question to Hugh, and he grinned at me dopily.

"He'll love it."

"You've seen Cameron since you've been back, too?" Mom's eyebrows raised, and she leaned back in her chair in a way that made me sit up straighter in mine. "You saw both your old boyfriends before us?"

"They're not my boyfriends," I instinctively retorted, instantly regretting it, and took a large, anxiety-fueled bite of cookie.

"Cameron was at the dinner last night, too, so we all caught up," Hugh tactfully explained.

Mom's face stormed over for a moment, but then she broke out into a huge smile. "I'm just messing with you, Muriel. You've got every right to catch up with old friends, and we always liked Cameron, didn't we, Mike?"

Dad wrinkled his nose slightly. "Nice boy, sure, but he's a bit too—" He waved his hands around like a hippy at Woodstock "—for me. I have no idea how he handles being a cop. No, I've always liked you best, Hugh." He winked at Hugh, who struggled to contain a huge grin.

"Cameron's sense of justice is incredible, Mr. Tennyson," Hugh replied. "His soft heart makes him a perfect cop. But Muriel's right, neither of us is her boyfriend."

Both of my parents' faces made it clear they didn't believe him, but they must have thought better of pressing any further. I breathed a sigh of relief as Dad changed the subject, addressing Hugh with an outstretched hand.

"By the way, I meant to thank you for reporting on the safety issues out at the lumber mill." The two men shook hands, and Hugh appeared genuinely touched by the gratitude.

Dad continued, "I used to work there back in the day, and I know what it's like there. You've helped out a lot of people; possibly saved lives even."

"Thanks, but I was just doing my job," Hugh replied humbly, and took a final swig of his Coke. "And on that subject, I'd better get back to it. There's a post-storm clean-up to report on. Is your landline working? I need to call a cab, and I still can't get a signal."

"I'll take you," I blurted out.

It had been a hell of a long day, leaving me so beyond tired that the thought of a bed made me woozy. But I didn't want to say goodbye to Hugh. I also hoped Cameron would be done with his shift soon so we could meet up again, although knowing him, he was probably going to work twenty-four hours straight to help out with the rescue effort.

My men were two good guys.

"You sure?" Hugh asked.

I nodded eagerly. "As long as I wouldn't be in the way. What do you plan to do, exactly?"

"Just drive around, see if I can help out anywhere. I'll do some interviews and take photos if people let me. Why?"

"I'd love to come along. You've got me all fired up and ready to help."

Chapter Thirteen
Muriel Tennyson

We said goodbye to my parents, but not before I promised to return for brunch the next day, which was fine. It had been fun to catch up with them, and Mom accepted Hugh's presence a lot more than I expected.

I realized she'd been a 'while you're under my roof' kind of parent. We were on a more equal level now that I was an adult with my own responsibilities. And of course, the fact that I'd managed to impress Patty and Beth didn't hurt, either.

Perhaps I'd been avoiding visiting my parents unnecessarily, and I had a lot of time to make up for once it sunk in that they weren't going to ground me for talking to boys.

All in all, the visit placed another tick in the 'Pros' column for returning to my hometown.

We headed back to Hugh's place, where I waited in the car while he got changed into some looser-fit clothes and grabbed some supplies. First-aid kit, a toolkit, and his police scanner; we were hopefully well-prepared to help out anyone who might need it.

"Mind if I switch on my scanner?" Hugh asked as we pulled away. "It's good for picking up where we might be most in need of help."

"Sure, go ahead."

He turned it on, and we drove for a while listening to the general buzz of cops updating each other over the radio. Suddenly, a familiar voice sounded out across the airwaves.

"Officers three-oh-one and five-seven-nine, code seven, Arburn, over."

A wave of fear surged through me, and I stared across at Hugh, wild-eyed.

"Code seven. What the hell is a code seven?"

Hugh laughed at my panic. "It's a lunch break, Muri, don't worry. Say, wanna see if we can meet up with him? We're not far from Arburn, and there's a waffle place he loves there. I bet that's where he'll be."

Panic turned to joy, and I agreed we should track him down. It had only been a few hours since we'd been with Cameron, but it seemed like ages, and I couldn't wait to see him again.

I followed Hugh's directions, and we arrived in just ten minutes. Sure enough, we found a cop car in the parking lot. We parked up, walked over, and peered through the window. Cameron was alone in the car and appeared to be drifting off in the driver's seat until I knocked at the window with a grin.

"Huh? Ah, wha—Muriel!" Cameron quickly came around and beamed when he saw Hugh and me standing outside his car. He rolled his window down, and I gave him a kiss. "What are you two doing here? Everything okay?"

"It's all good; we just had an idea about joining you for lunch."

"Hah, I wish." Cam unlocked the back door of the car so we could climb inside. "The waffle place is shut. Which is totally reasonable given that it... well, it doesn't really have a roof anymore," He gestured to the devastated building. "But I just wanted a waffle so bad I can taste it. Does that sound selfish?"

"Yes," Hugh said flatly, before breaking out into a smile. "But you're doing a hard job today; you're entitled to be a bit selfish."

"They're well insured, anyway. I remember helping them with some tips on security measures they put in place and those things helped lower the cost of their insurance. Still, it might be a long time before they serve another waffle."

"I make waffles." I patted Cameron's shoulder reassuringly. "How about you come over to my parents' house tomorrow, and I'll make you all some?"

Cameron turned around in his seat, clearly surprised by the offer. "You're inviting us to meet your parents? Or are you going to have us dress up like Poppy and Jas so they don't realize it's us?"

"Somehow, I don't think you two can get away with that." I giggled, looking at the strapping, broad-shouldered men.

It was so good to be close to them both again, and the electricity that sparked in the air when we were all together was definitely still there.

"We've already visited Muri's parents earlier today. They definitely suspect something more than friendship is going on, and they almost seemed encouraging about it?"

My nose scrunched up automatically. "No. Well, I'm sure my dad would be happy with me dating you, Hugh, and my mom clearly likes you." I gestured toward Cameron, who smiled widely and stuck his tongue out at Hugh. "But I don't think they could even comprehend that all three of us might be together."

"I don't know," Hugh said thoughtfully. "I got the impression they suspected something close to the truth, and since I wasn't banished from the house forever, they might be okay with it."

I wanted to argue but had to admit that he might be right.

While I still wasn't sure my mom even knew anything about the concept of three-way relationships, there was something in the way my parents spoke that suggested they were happy for me, no matter what my situation.

Perhaps the speech I'd been mentally preparing, where I tell them that it's my life and I'm not their little girl anymore, would remain unsaid. The idea was liberating and a little scary.

"Where's Vic?" Hugh asked.

"He's gone for a walk. Apparently, he was sick of hearing about waffles and needed some space away from me. Say, that gives me an idea..."

Cameron stepped out of the car, and Hugh and I gave each other quizzical looks as he walked around to the back door.

"Shuffle up," he said, climbing inside next to me. "And whatever happens, this door must stay open or we'll be locked inside until Vic comes back and rescues us."

It was cramped in the back, and the proximity to the two guys made me heat up despite the breeze through the open door.

Cameron grinned wickedly at both of us. "I've always wanted to get frisky in my car."

"Cameron!" I called out, laughing at the suggestion. "I'm pretty sure that's not legal." It wasn't an objection on my account; in fact, the idea appealed immensely, but I didn't want anyone to get in trouble.

"What do you mean? I'm on my break, the scanner's still running in case of an emergency, and I'm pretty sure frisking a woman isn't illegal, if she consents to it."

Hugh narrowed his eyes at his friend. "You worry me sometimes, you know. Indecent exposure? And I'm willing to bet there are regulations, at least, against cops having sex on the job."

"Hugh, must you live so relentlessly on the straight and narrow? There's nobody around, my break isn't over for another half hour, and isn't Muri looking more gorgeous than ever right now?"

"Are there cameras in here?" I asked.

"Yes, but I'll only switch them on if you want a copy of the video," Cameron waggled his eyebrows.

"No, thank you." I laughed, although the idea did have a certain appeal. I began to stroke the inner thighs of both my men. My legs parted slightly, seemingly of their own accord. I was more than ready and willing to give Cameron what he wanted.

When my hand reached the tent that had already formed in Hugh's pants, his face flushed slightly, and he licked his lips. "Fuck it, fine."

Cameron kissed me then, and I twisted and turned to put my legs up on the seat, leaning back against Hugh and reaching up to run my fingers through his curly hair.

Cameron's kiss was hard and hungry, and clearly he needed to blow off steam after his day of being a hero. His hand tickled the underside of my right knee before it started moving achingly slowly up my thigh and beneath my skirt.

I gasped as his fingers brushed the thin layer of cotton that separated me from him. I threw my head back against Hugh's chest, and Hugh responded by moving his hands underneath my sweater. He pulled up my top, exposing my breasts completely.

My back arched as Hugh touched my breasts, teasing my nipples and watching me squirm with delight.

Once again, I found myself not caring if any passers-by saw me that way.

Cameron pulled at my panties, and I lifted my hips to let him remove them completely. He threw them on the floor, and in an instant his fingers slipped into me with no resistance. Skillfully he teased and fingered me until they had me almost sobbing with pleasure.

Hugh kept on playing with my sensitive nipples while looking down in apparent awe at my exposed body in front of him.

"You are fucking sexy." Cameron's voice was husky and low. His breathing heavy.

He upped the pace, fucking me hard with his fingers: long and hard like I didn't need anything else but his hands.

Together they hit all my right notes perfectly as if they knew my body better than they should after such a short time.

I bucked and moaned as the shock of a fast and sudden climax moved through me, engulfing from head to toe.

Pleasure shot through my body, reverberating around for what seemed like an eternity. Spots appeared in my vision, and I thought I might blackout until eventually the sensations finally began to recede.

Cameron withdrew his hand, raised his fingers to his face and proceeded to sniff them before licking each one.

It would have been mortifyingly embarrassing, except he looked like he was in heaven and eating a great delicacy.

"You taste so fucking good," he said with that adorable boyish grin of his. "That was nice."

"Nice. That's an understatement," I replied, still catching my breath. "Now, what can I do for y'all?"

The had me so wound up and turned on I'd have done anything for them right then.

"Ah, we'd better leave it there and not push our luck." Hugh looking out of the window. But even with his cautious attitude he didn't conceal the huge, tempting bulge in his pants. "Vic or anyone else might come by any minute."

"Aww," I pouted, brattishly. "But I really want to."

"Hugh's right, and anyway the sight and scent and flavor of you is more than enough for me," Cameron grinned while adjusting himself. "That'll keep me going the rest of my shift."

A buzz started emanating in my jacket pocket, and we all looked down at the floor in surprise. My phone. They must have got a mast repaired somewhere. I fished it out and my agent's photo flashed up on the screen.

"Sorry, I have to take this." I stepped out of the car, picking up my panties on the way. I did *not* want Vic finding those.

"Hello?"

"Muriel!" Alexa screamed down the phone. "I've been trying to get hold of you. For. So. Long. What's going on?"

"Long story, but short version, I've been stuck in a storm for the past day." I paced around the parking lot, looking back at Cameron's car and admiring my men, who animatedly chatted away.

"Oh, you poor baby. Well, this will cheer you up. You know Hulu, the streaming people?"

"Uh, huh." I loved Alexa, but for some reason she always spoke to me like I was a country bumpkin. Probably because she was Los Angeles born and raised, and I was a recent import.

"Well, they're looking for an influencer-type girl to have her own reality series. You know, a girl about town in LA; her life, love, style, all that crap." Alexa paused for a moment. "And they want you, Muriel Tennyson. You. They love your Instagram; they say your personality just shines through everything you do, and you would be a perfect fit for their audience."

"Huh." I should have had more to say, but in truth, I was stunned. An offer like that was a dream come true... wasn't it?

"I know, I was lost for words too. And look, their offer isn't the best, but it's not bad for a first series, and I'm sure I can get them up from two hundred grand, at least a little—"

"What, what?" I stuttered.

"Yeah, I reckon two-fifty is realistic, really. And you'd get all kinds of sponsorships from this, probably a free car, that kind of thing. How excited are you?"

Two hundred thousand dollars. I made decent money in my influencing work, but student loans still hung heavily over my head, and in lean months, I struggled to pay rent on my dollhouse-sized apartment.

I only had to let cameras follow me around and join in with the whole 'one drama an episode, neatly wrapped up by the end' thing. It would be too easy. Except for one thing...

"You say they want the show to cover my love life? Isn't that a bit private?"

"Oh, sweetie." If it were possible, I sensed Alexa pouting condescendingly down the phone. "That's the whole point. Haven't you seen the Kardashians' show? But they're billionaires, Muri. Billion. Aires. People want to see how you live your life—the good, the bad, and the ugly."

I looked back at Hugh and Cameron.

Would the producers walk away if I mentioned the throuple? Or worse, would they rub their hands with glee, knowing people will pay the monthly fee just to watch Muriel and the circus freak show?

"Look, it's amazing. Incredible. But I have to take time to think about it. I fly back to LA in a couple of days, and I'll give you a call when I get back, okay?"

"No. The producers want to have dinner with you tomorrow. Don't mess this up, Muri—if you get this job, you'll be able to get a private jet back to Georgia whenever you want, so get your cute little tushie back here right now."

"Okay, Alexa, I get it. Bye."

I hung up, imagining the look of shock my agent must be wearing. Any other girl on her books would have been dancing around and screaming like a banshee.

I couldn't help but feel ungrateful. But it was more complicated for me; much more. I decided not to tell the boys, and I plastered on a casual smile as I headed back to the car, and my brain throbbed as I tried to figure out a solution.

"Everything okay?" Hugh asked as I got back into the car. "You're beet red."

"Yes, fine. Do you blame me for being flushed after what we just did?" I lied. "The call was just my agent. She found... an umbrella in her office, and she wondered if it's mine. It isn't. I don't own an umbrella. The one she found was white."

Dammit, Muriel, learn how to lie.

"Uh huh," Hugh muttered.

"Cool story." Cameron said playfully as if he didn't believe a word of it but didn't mind one bit. "Well, here's Vic now."

"We'll let you get on then," Hugh said. "We're going to drive around for the evening, see if there's anyone that needs help."

"You're good people," Cameron said, at which I experienced a pang of guilt.

"Hey, I wondered whether instead of going to your parents' tomorrow, you would both like to come over to mine, maybe around six? No pressure, Muriel," he said, holding his hands up innocently.

"That would be awesome." In truth, I didn't know whether I'd even still be in Georgia by the following evening, but I wouldn't turn down an invitation to some more private time with my guys. Why couldn't my heart and my brain ever be on the same side?

Chapter Fourteen
Muriel Tennyson

We drove out to Ashford, and while Hugh used the newly working mobile signal to phone contacts and find out more about the storm, I spent the time reflecting on my situation.

Being offered my own TV show was insane. Like, completely nuts. Out of all the wannabes in LA, a major producer had chosen *me. A*nd I absolutely considered myself as a wannabe.

Money aside, did I really want to do it?

Even without the complication of Hugh and Cameron, it would be a huge deal, putting my life on display for millions of people to watch and discuss. Like everyone, I'd heard horror stories about reality TV stars getting edited to look bad and becoming hated overnight.

Also, it didn't excite me like it should.

If it was the right thing to do, surely I'd be as excited by it as by the prospect of doing fundraising for storm victims?

Still, I couldn't pretend the money wasn't significant. I could *not* afford to dismiss two hundred grand out of hand.

Most importantly of all, I had to remember my long-term goal of having my own designer clothing label. There'd be no better opportunity to promote myself; I could even make up some designs and wear them on the show.

I tried to imagine what Poppy and Jasmine would say if I asked them what I should do, but it was too easy and totally unanimous: "Do the show, stupid."

"What has got you deep in silent contemplation?" Hugh looked over at me with a curious expression.

"Oh, nothing," I said, trying to act casual. "Just looking forward to tomorrow, is all."

He beamed in response. "Yeah, it'll be fun." Hugh put his arm on my shoulder, and I leaned back against it, comforted by his touch. "I'm glad you're going to be here more often. And with your folks being so chill about things, I'm actually surprisingly hopeful for once in my life."

I laughed, but it was hollow.

Hugh had faith in something for once, while I weighed up whether to crush it.

As we drove through the streets, evidence of the devastation of the storm became more and more clear. I was incredibly grateful that my parents' area had barely been affected.

We stopped in a street where almost every house had been damaged in some way, and Hugh jumped out with his notebook and camera.

"Don't you have a photographer at the paper?"

He laughed ruefully. "I'm not at the LA Times, remember. I have to do all my own spell checking, too."

He walked around taking photos, and I decided to do the same, figuring that I should post them on my Instagram as part of my campaign.

Houses with broken windows and debris strewn all about were all around.

As I took pictures of a half-collapsed house that was buckling under the weight of a fallen oak tree, a hand wrapped around my waist, and Hugh pulled me in tight, his body against my back. His chin rested on my shoulder. "Holy shit, that's a beautiful photo."

"Er, it's not supposed to be beautiful, Hugh. It's sad. A family's home has been destroyed."

"Sad things can be beautiful too," he pointed out and kissed my ear. "And anyway, I'm just saying that you're a good photographer. I can understand why you're so successful on social media, even if I've never got to see your posts."

I laughed, leaning back against him. It seemed like a lifetime ago that I blocked them, when I was a whole different person. My eyebrow raised as a certain something pressed against my ass, and I looked up with a coy smile.

"I didn't know you liked photography that much, Mr. Davis," I teased, and he blushed, running his hand through his messy, curly hair.

"I mean, it depends on the photograph—"

"Hey, Hugh." Someone interrupted him mid-sentence, calling over from the other side of the street. A middle-aged man, balding and clearly in some distress, paced over toward us. He was clearly pleased to see Hugh.

"Jason." Hugh let me go and walked over to the man, adjusting his pants as he walked, although I suspected there was no hiding that bulge. I followed, not wanting to seem rude, and Jason met me with a firm, hearty handshake.

"This is Muriel. Muri, this is Jason, our old IT guy at the paper."

"Ah, Muriel. I've heard a lot about you," Jason said, and I noticed Hugh attempt to subtly stop him talking by waving his hand across his throat. It wasn't subtle, and it didn't work. "You're some sort of LA big-shot, aren't you? A model, is it?"

"Not really a model." When the man looked confused, I added, "But something like that. Nice to meet you."

"Hugh used to talk about you a lot. Said you were the cutest girl in high school and the funniest person full stop. And he still owes me five dollars that I lent him on my last day at the paper, which is why I'm telling you this." The man grinned evilly.

Hugh groaned. "For Christ's sake, Jase, here you go." Hugh pulled a wallet out of his jeans, but Jason waved it away.

"I'm only messing with you, Hugh. To tell you the truth, five dollars wouldn't get me very far at the moment; that's my house you were taking pictures of." He waved over at the devastated house.

I suddenly felt a little guilty. "I'm so sorry." I stared at the house in dismay.

"No, not that one. The next one along with the smashed windows." He waved his hand dismissively. "Don't be sorry about it. It's our fault, we decided we were smarter than The Weather Channel, and it seems we've paid the price."

"A lot of people appear to have done the same," Hugh said, and I nodded.

Chrissy, for one, and I wondered how she was dealing with the disappointment of her wedding not going ahead.

"Mind if I ask you a few questions for the paper? I'll help you get the house wind and watertight at the same time, if you want."

"Yeah, that sounds good. Let me introduce my kids, too; they're out the back trying to board up some windows." Jason turned and headed toward the house.

Hugh bent down to speak in a lower voice for only me to hear. "Sorry about that. I didn't talk about you that much in the office, I promise."

"Hey, you'd hear far worse if you asked Poppy and Jasmine what I say about you," I reassured him. "In far more graphic language too, I'm certain."

He laughed. "I'd like to ask them. We'll all have to go out for dinner sometime."

A pang of anxiety hit me. A night out with my boys *and* my girls would be heaven, once the girls had gotten past the initial shock and questions about the throuple arrangement. But with a film crew trailing behind us? No. I couldn't let that nightmare happen.

I left Hugh with his old colleague and took the opportunity to get some fresh air, taking photos as I wandered through the nearby streets. I helped out wherever possible, removing dangerous debris from the roads and clearing up the shattered glass before anyone stepped in it.

The sights surrounding me and the clear-up activities made me appreciate only having my problems. Two hundred grand or two handsome men who were also sweet, kind and in work; things could be so much worse.

"Help. Help."

A high-pitched voice snapped me out of my thoughts, and I looked around until I noticed a very young girl waving her arm at me desperately. I ran over, and on seeing she was crying, I instinctively wrapped an arm around her.

"It's all right, darlin'," I said soothingly. "What's wrong?"

"Mommy is stuck," she cried. "Underground. Please help." I took her hand, and she led me around the back of her house. "Here."

The entrance to a storm shelter on the ground was open, but almost completely covered in the siding that had fallen from the neighboring building.

The kid ran up and stuck her hand toward the tiny gap left, and her mother's fingers emerged from it.

"It's okay, baby, it's all right," a tired voice emanated from the shelter. I kneeled beside the child, placing an arm around her for added reassurance.

"Hello?"

"Oh, hi there. How ya doin'?" the voice from the shelter called out.

"I'm... I'm fine. I'm more worried about you. Do you have any other way out, through the main house maybe?"

"If I did, I wouldn't be standing here on a ladder with my fingers sticking out of the ground like a zombie coming back to life now, would I?"

I recognized that voice, and that sarcastic banter. "Zoe?"

"That's me. Say, is that Muriel?"

"It is." We were old, good-natured foes from volleyball. I hadn't heard from her since we left school.

"Well, this is a weird way to meet up after so long. Say, any chance you can find someone to help me out of here? I've been in here for hours, and I don't want to have to pis— pee in a bucket again if I can help it."

"Sure, give me a minute, and I'll see what I can do."

I called Hugh. He'd managed to gather a small group of men to help secure Jason's house; once they were done, they'd come straight over to rescue Zoe. I went back to tell her and her daughter the good news.

"Oooh, Hugh?" Zoe said, and I cursed the fact that small-town gossip was so powerful it was deemed even more important than life-or-death rescue attempts. "I didn't know you two were a thing still. I heard you headed off to California to make your fortune."

I forced out a smile to appease the distressed little girl who sat next to me. "Not exactly a fortune, but I am living out in LA. Hugh and I are just friends; I came into town for Chrissy's wedding."

There it was again: the denial—just friends. I felt terrible for saying it.

"Friends, uh-huh." She used a wry tone that made me bristle. "And who was that other one you were always with... Ryan, was it?"

"Cameron," I corrected her. "Yeah, just friends with him too."

There was a long, sarcastic sigh. "I believe you, Muri, and thousands wouldn't."

"Girls and boys can be just friends, you do know that?"

I was caught between wanting to head back out on my own, avoiding this sort of questioning, and a sense of obligation to help Zoe, who was clearly in distress. The right thing to do was to stay, so I tried to nudge the conversation in a different direction.

"Your daughter here is beautiful," I said, and the little girl smiled for the first time since I'd met her. "And brave too, going out to find help. You are very lucky."

"Oh, Marie's a doll," Zoe replied, squeezing her free fingers against the little girl's hand. "You'll remember her dad, Ralph?"

"Aw, Ralphie?" I remembered the adorable little boy in class who used to almost pee his pants every time anyone asked him a question.

"Yeah. Weren't you two in math together? Well, anyway, he got me knocked up not long after we finished high school, and now here we are."

"That's sweet," I said. I wasn't particularly impressed with Zoe's turn of phrase in front of her daughter, but my job here was to stop either of them from going into panic mode before the cavalry arrived. "I hope I get what you have someday."

"You can have it right now, I reckon," Zoe replied. "Word around town is those two boys haven't stopped pining over you since you left."

My eyes were in danger of rolling right out of my head. Oh, for Christ's sake, was there no real news in this place?

Why would some random girl I used to throw a ball at years ago have as much information about my own love life as I did?. But that was small-town life. The downside of everybody knowing your name was that everybody knew your business too.

I wondered whether Zoe knew about Cameron and Hugh sharing women before; did she know Hannah? My cheeks flushed with shame.

"I'm not so sure about that." I tried to laugh off Zoe's suggestion.

Before she had a chance to pry any further, I caught a glimpse of Hugh walking toward us with a group of men behind him, like a superhero arriving at the last possible moment.

"The rescue squad's here," I called out, and Marie squealed with excitement.

"They're going to get Mommy out."

"Yes, they are." I clapped my hands to match the little girl's energy.

"Hey," Hugh said as he arrived. "This doesn't seem so bad; we'll have your mommy out in just a minute, okay?"

Marie nodded, and Hugh offered his fist for her to bump.

I swear my ovaries twitched for the first time in my life, but I chose to ignore the sensation. I had enough going on without adding a baby into the mix, thank you very much.

Hugh gathered the men around the large pieces of siding that blocked Zoe's exit. I grabbed a section too and encouraged Marie to do the same so she'd feel like she helped her mom.

One by one, we heaved the large pieces of siding aside, and eventually we got the entrance uncovered so Zoe could climb out.

She seemed shaky, but pretty good considering the ordeal she'd been through the past few hours. She gratefully accepted a water bottle from one of the rescuers, and then came over to give me a hug.

"Thanks for helping me and Marie, hon. I'd have been in there for the night ahead if it wasn't for you."

"It was nothing, really," I replied.

She took me by the shoulder earnestly. "I meant what I said, you know? That guy's nuts about you." She gestured over at Hugh, who was busy piling wood into a pickup. "And that Ryan guy is, too..."

"Cameron," I corrected her again.

She waved her hand in the air dismissively. "Whatever. I don't care what his name is, but you do, and that's the main thing. Go for it, Muriel; trust me."

Chapter Fifteen
Muriel Tennyson

Zoe's daughter was calling for her, so she gave me a final shoulder squeeze and headed over to see her, leaving me speechless.

"You okay?" Hugh sidled up beside me. Beads of sweat had formed on his brow, and streaks of mud and old paint were smeared all over him, making him appear more heroic than a local journalist had any right to.

"I'm fine," I replied uncertainly. "Say, does Zoe know that you and Cameron dated Hannah?"

Hugh shrugged. "Dunno. Maybe. Why?"

"Just something she said, that's all."

"Oookay. Well, Jason gave me some sandwiches, and they look pretty damn good. How about we eat them, then drive around a bit more and call it a night?"

I agreed, and we headed back to the car.

Hugh wrapped his arm around me as we walked, and I did the same, leaning my head on his arm.

I wished that Cameron was walking on the other side of me, making us complete. It was quite an incredible realization that if he were here, snuggled up to me as close as Hugh was, someone like Zoe might not even bat an eyelid.

But not everyone was like Zoe, I reasoned, remembering the boys' run-in with Elijah. And if I did the TV show, the complaints from the Elijahs of the world would outweigh anything the Zoes had to say, probably fifty to one.

It was too much to process, yet I really needed to decide urgently if I had a hope of catching a flight back to LA first thing the next morning. There was only one thing for it; a good old-fashioned pros and cons list.

Hugh grabbed the sandwiches from the trunk of the car, and we walked a few blocks until we reached the edge of the park. He lay his jacket on a park bench, which was quite pointless since the jacket was probably wetter and filthier than the bench, but I appreciated the gesture.

The scene in front of us was not idyllic, since fallen trees littered the park and there was even a collapsed electricity pylon directly in front of us, but with the sun low in the sky and a handsome man by my side it was kind of romantic, in a way.

"A dystopian romance," Hugh commented, as if reading my mind. I turned and kissed him, our lips melding into each other for a few moments before he gently pulled away.

"If we keep doing that, Cameron'll get jealous." He grinned.

"Would he really?" It hadn't occurred to me before, but now I wondered about the logistics of a three-way relationship. Would I have to make sure I gave each guy an equal half of my attention? Should we only get intimate if we were all together?

"Nah, I'm just kidding. If we do end up making this official, there's going to be times one of us is with you more than the other; that's life. He'll be happy to know I'm with you when he can't be."

"Phew, I was starting to worry about having to do admin to keep things straight."

Hugh laughed. "Like a sex ledger? That would take the fun out of things, wouldn't it?"

"Just a bit. No one wants more paperwork."

We finished our sandwiches as the last rays of sunshine fell below the horizon.

After a few minutes of silence, I turned to find Hugh slumped against the bench, fast asleep. I didn't blame him; it had been the longest, weirdest day of my life, and I hadn't spent the last couple of hours doing essential construction work.

Determined to let him nap for a little while longer, I pulled out my phone. Bringing up the Notes app, I started to list out my options and their implications; there was nothing like seeing your problems in black and white to get your problem-solving juices flowing.

So, option one was becoming a throuple.

Pros: Hot sex, time in at home, hopefully get to see my parents more often.

Cons: Couldn't do TV show, Hugh's mom, judgments from people around town, just a bit weird?

Option two, flying back to LA in the morning to meet the producers.

Pros: Money ($200k...), a head-start on my designer career, free stuff.

I sarcastically put an asterisk around free stuff; Jas would tell me to make that my number one consideration. I loved her to bits, but in some ways, she was barely human.

Cons: Couldn't be with Hugh & Cameron.

"What you up to?" I jumped as Hugh placed his hand on my thigh. Quickly, I locked my phone and shoved it in my pocket before turning back to him with an innocent smile.

"Nothing, only a grocery list. Ready to go? Sleepyhead needs his bed."

Hugh yawned, stretching his toned arms over his head as he did so. "You're right there. I'm an old man now; I can't stay out too late."

"Hey. Less of the 'old,' please." I swatted him playfully in the chest. "We're the same age, remember?"

"Ah, well, women age at a different rate than men, you see..."

His attempt to dig himself out of the hole made me laugh, and I grabbed his hand and hauled him up to stop him from saying any more.

The car was only a short walk away, thankfully, as I needed to get back to my list and finally make a decision.

Almost as soon as we climbed inside, Hugh started to fall asleep again. I clicked my fingers in front of his face to wake him.

"Hey, hey. I don't exactly remember how to get back to your place? Unless you want to go back to your parents?"

"No way. I've had enough of my mom for one day, thanks. Just head along this road for a couple of miles; I'll tell you where to turn." I started to wonder about the inside of Hugh's apartment; I imagined it all white with a few tasteful monochrome photos dotted around the walls.

"Right, I'm going to need some of that crappy music you like if I'm going to stay awake." He grabbed my phone from the dashboard before I managed to stop him. "I got to tell you, it's really bad not to have a passcode on your phone. You'd better hope there aren't nudes on here for some scumbag to ste— hey, what's this?"

I turned to see Hugh's face become steely and serious, and I instantly knew I'd left the Notes app up.

"That's private. Put it down."

"My name's on here, and my mom's."

"It's nothing; it's just—"

"What's this TV show, Muri?"

I gritted my teeth, furious that he'd read the list when I told him not to. Of course, if I stumbled across a note like that with my name on it, there wasn't a chance in hell I wouldn't read it too, but being angry was easier than dealing with my guilt.

"It's none of your business."

"I repeat, my name is on here, as well as Cameron's." He spoke calmly, which only made me more flustered. "Just tell me what's going on."

"It's... I've been offered the chance to do a reality show in LA," I admitted.

"La-di-da," Hugh said sarcastically.

"And it would be the chance of a lifetime, except the producers want access to every area of my life—"

"—and you wouldn't want the world to know about us?"

I sighed. "I don't know. I guess not. Do you blame me?"

He shrugged. "Turn here."

I did as I was told while fighting off the tears that threatened to make my night vision even worse.

"There's no way you'd be getting me on a shitty TV show, so your dirty little secret would be safe, anyway. But after the day we've just spent together, why didn't you tell me about this?"

"I did think about it, I... there's a lot on my mind."

"Clearly. I can see here that you have to weigh up hot sex versus money and *free stuff*."

He spat out those last words with a level of disdain I'd never heard from him before.

"It's not like that, Hugh. The list isn't finished. You woke up before I—"

"Oh, I'm so sorry for waking up."

Goddammit, this man's sarcasm would be the death of me.

"You woke up before I finished the list. It's how I work things through in my head, and you really shouldn't have snooped, anyway."

"Yeah, well, I've paid the price for it, haven't I? You have no idea how close I came to telling my mom about you today?"

I snorted. "You're a twenty-three-year-old man, Hugh; I'm not going to be impressed by you telling your mom about a girlfriend."

"You aren't my girlfriend," he replied, not sarcastically or with anger this time, only sadness. "Your a woman who isn't sure if she'd prefer *free stuff* or hot sex."

My tears started to flow for real, and my hand couldn't wipe them away fast enough. My driving slowed to a crawl.

"When do you go back to LA?"

"I haven't decided to go back yet."

"When?"

I sniffed back a sob. "Tomorrow morning."

"Cameron's expecting you tomorrow night."

I didn't have a response. I should have told them everything when Cameron invited me, but I didn't, for reasons I couldn't even remember. We drove in silence except for the occasional direction until Hugh started to play with his police scanner.

"I need to tell Cameron what's going on; I'll find out if he's finished his shift yet."

"No, I'll tell him."

"It'd be better coming from me; he's used to me bumming him out."

The scanner crackled into life, and there was a flurry of activity. It was not surprising that the rescue efforts from the storm were still underway, but it did seem a little too active for this time of night.

"I repeat: Code three, P-two, Ebbs Way and Turner. Officers three-oh-one and five-seven-nine trapped in car; condition unknown. Over."

I sucked in a breath, hard. "Those numbers... aren't they—"

"Yes." Hugh gripped his car seat so tightly he was in danger of tearing the upholstery clear off. "We have to go to him."

"Won't we get in the way? I mean—"

"Go now. Junction of Ebbs Way and Turner Avenue."

My body responded naturally to his surprisingly calm yet commanding tone. I turned the car around with a screech on the empty road.

"Those codes they were using, the three and the P-two, what do they mean?"

"Nothing good," Hugh replied.

Chapter Sixteen
Hugh Davis

He'll be okay. He has to be okay.

Muriel raced through the streets as fast as she could while dodging the debris that remained in the road.

He will be fine.

We would probably arrive on the scene to find Cameron sipping chicken soup and laughing at some dumb joke. He'd give me a playful punch in the arm for being worried about him, and Muriel would tell us her gross little list was a meaningless stupid prank, and she wanted nothing better than to be with us.

A list she hadn't finished.

I told myself that, but I didn't believe a word of it.

"Are you telling yourself everything is going to be fine, by any chance?" Muriel asked, glancing at me from the corner of her eye as she drove.

"Yup," I replied.

She nodded slowly. "Same. That's what Cameron would be doing if it was either of us, so perhaps by matching his... I dunno, vibes? Perhaps that'll help."

That was a load of horseshit, but I knew better than to say anything. If it made Muriel feel better to think Cameron would be safe if we believed hard enough, then I'd go along with that for her sake. And I wished it were true too.

"That was pure crap I just said, wasn't it?" she said, and despite everything, I had to laugh.

"Total nonsense," I agreed, and then gripped the dashboard as Muriel swerved around an abandoned car in the road.

The streetlights were out in this area, making the situation even more dangerous. I easily understood how Cameron and Vic got into trouble, despite being experienced, highly skilled drivers.

We arrived on-scene to find a bunch of firefighters sitting around their truck, with Cameron and Vic still stuck upside down in the car being tended to by paramedics.

It seemed they'd swerved to avoid being hit by a collapsing building, and they ended up being hit by it, anyway. The scene was a total mess. I was relieved to see Cameron and Vic moving with my own eyes, otherwise I wouldn't have believed there were any survivors in the car.

Muriel ran straight to Cameron and crouched down to hold his hand through the broken window. I strode over to the fire truck, ready to explode with anger.

"What the hell are you doing, standing around doing nothing?"

"Wrong equipment, buddy. They need cutting out of there. We're waiting on another truck now."

I shook my head in disbelief. "How the hell don't you have the right equip— never mind. How long will the truck be?"

One of the firefighters shrugged. "Soon, we hope. We're spread thin because of the storm."

I took a deep breath, trying to see things from their perspective. They couldn't magic the right equipment onto the scene, and times were tough for the emergency services at that moment.

"Hey, you're Hugh Davis, aren't you?" someone called out from the truck. I peered inside.

"Er, yeah?"

"I'm Lieutenant Chuck Helmsley. You wrote that article for the *Chronicle* about how we're underfunded, didn't you?"

I'd almost forgotten about that. I'd written it up last year. Fat lot of good it did, apparently. "Yeah, that was me."

"Thanks for doing that, bud. Things move slowly at City Hall."

I snorted; that was an understatement.

"But next year's budget is looking a lot healthier."

Well, that was something. I didn't have time for self-satisfaction, though; my best friend was stuck and bleeding. An EMT attempted to bandage his wound while he was still in the car, but it was clearly a struggle.

"I'm glad to hear it," I called out. "Say, is there anything you can do to at least find out when the truck will get here? That's my best friend in there, and his partner."

"Let me give them a call," Chuck said.

I headed straight over to the upturned patrol car.

"Hugh," Cameron said weakly as I arrived. "How's it going?"

"Better for me than you, champ," I replied.

Champ? Stress was making me say some strange things.

Cameron didn't seem to mind, and he smiled broadly.

"Ah, this is nothing. I'll be right as rain as soon as they get me out of here—aargh."

"Sorry." The EMT said, having pressed a little too heavily on Cameron's head wound. "Look, it's kind of crowded here. Can you two give me some space, please?"

She was quite right; Muriel held Cameron's hand, and I was as close to him as I could get, making access difficult for the only person who could practically do anything for him right now.

I stood up and touched Muriel's shoulder to encourage her to step away.

"Thanks. I'll let you know as soon as I'm done."

We walked behind the vehicle, and I leaned back on a tree in exhaustion. "How does he seem?"

"Upbeat, obviously," Muriel replied. "But he can't feel his legs. That's never good, is it?" Her eyes filled with fresh tears.

"Not usually," I admitted, and her face fell even further. This wasn't the time for my plain speaking. "But miracles happen all the time." Who I was trying to convince more, her or myself? I wasn't doing a good job with either.

"You sound like Cameron." Muriel laughed through her tears, and despite everything that had happened, I wrapped my arms around her and pulled her into my chest. My heart pounded against her ear, and she relaxed against my body as I slowly stroked her hair.

"I'm sorry," she said quietly.

"It's okay," I lied.

After a few minutes, Muriel's sobs had receded, and she stood up straight, wiping her face dry. "Ugh, I'm being ridiculous. I never cry."

"This isn't a normal situation you're dealing with," I said reassuringly, and she looked up at me, smiling.

"You're right. Are you going to tell Cameron what happened tonight?"

I rolled my eyes, hard. "Oh yes, that would be great, wouldn't it? 'Hey buddy, while you're hanging there upside down with a gaping head wound, here's some disappointing news for ya...' I'm not a monster, Muriel."

"I know you're not. You're just a little obsessed with the truth, sometimes."

Fair point.

"Just this once, I'll err on the side of sensitivity. Do me a favor, though, don't mislead him about anything, okay? Don't tell him you want to be with us to make him feel better, because I'm the one who'll have to pick up the pieces. It'd be like taking a bone away from an injured puppy."

Muriel smiled. "I can do that."

"Hey, you two. I'm done over here if you want to keep Cameron company."

We walked over, and as I passed, she tapped me on the shoulder and muttered, "Just to warn you, he might be delirious; he's talking non-stop about waffles and nineties boy bands."

"Oh, good," I said, and she appeared taken aback. "That's standard Cameron, it means he's fine. I'd only be worried if he *wasn't* talking gibberish."

The EMT nodded with a smile and left us with him.

We sat back down on the cold wet ground and peered in at our friends.

"How're you doing over there, Vic?" I called out, and got a thumbs-up in response.

"It's the wedding day I'd always dreamed of."

Vic had gotten away without any real injuries, just a few bruises, but the car had rolled onto Cameron's side, so he'd taken the brunt of the accident.

"Don't worry. I'll stare out of my window and let you lovebirds catch up."

Cameron laughed before clutching his ribs in pain. "Ow. Right, I officially can't laugh. Thanks though, Vic."

I sneaked a glance at Muriel. She was blushing hard; I wasn't sure whether it was guilt about the fact that she was probably leaving us, or embarrassment that Vic knew about us. Neither option was encouraging for me, but I let it lie for now.

"So, you're still coming tomorrow night?" Cameron asked cheerfully.

Muriel was about to answer, but I didn't want to risk her committing to anything, so I interrupted immediately.

"Let's get tonight over with first, all right? For all we know, you might be getting a few days' vacation in the hospital."

"Nah, I told you I'm fine," he protested, but his face told a different story and that was only what he wanted to believe.

"We'll play it by ear, right? Say, remember when we were kids, and we'd have contests to find out who could hang upside down from the monkey bars the longest?"

Cameron and Muriel both nodded, laughing at the memory.

"All training for this moment. And I'll belatedly take the trophy for that now," Cameron said.

"For once, I won't argue with you on that," I replied.

"Hey, see ho— Ohh," Cameron's expression suddenly changed, as his face instantly paled and his eyes rolled around in his head.

"Help!" Muriel screamed, leaping up to get someone's attention. "Help, something's gone wrong."

I gripped Cameron's hand as he lost consciousness, and tears welled up in my eyes. Seeing him like this was torture.

He was my brother from a different mother. I talked to him about things that I never discussed with anyone. He knew my innermost thoughts in a way that no one else did. He got me and I got him in the same way.

"Come on, don't do this," I muttered under my breath. "You can't leave me. Leave us."

I was still holding Cameron's limp hand when a fire truck careened around the corner. I swung my head round to see two firefighters running toward me with hydraulic rescue tools, and I gave Cameron's hand a final squeeze before jumping out of the way to make room for them.

Muriel and I watched as they made light work of cutting the car open.

She stood in front of me, and I wrapped my arms around her, giving her reassuring pecks on the top of her head that she leaned into me with sorrowful sighs.

As soon as he was free, the EMTs were ready with a backboard and gurney to whisk him into the ambulance.

"I'm going to go to the hospital and wait. Will you drop me off at my place so I can get my car?"

She turned around with an offended expression on her face.

"I'm coming to the hospital too."

"Are you sure? I mean—"

"I'm going whether you like it or not. Our conversation about my plans isn't finished, and you aren't going to stop me from seeing Cameron."

I held my hands up in surrender. "Okay, okay. Fine. I believe you were dangerously close to saying you would go to his house before, and we agreed you wouldn't."

"Oh, go to hell, Hugh. I care about him, and he was in distress. You aren't the boss of me, right?"

I gritted my teeth. Was she right? Would it have been better to reassure Cameron for now? Say everything was fine between us all? And even if not, was it my place to tell her what she could say to him? I had no idea; lines were blurring all over the place.

"I'm sorry, okay? I'm just protective over Cameron; you know that. Now, let's get to the hospital."

Chapter Seventeen
Muriel Tennyson

It was all too much, and I was at my breaking point.

Never in my life had I snapped at Hugh before; needled him, yes, teased him, absolutely. But to hear him suggest that I might not want to be with Cameron when he needed me the most offended me to my very core.

How dare Hugh try to police what I say to Cam? Just because he was brainy and a hero around town, it didn't mean I gave two hoots about his opinion on everything.

Except, I did.

And deep down, I knew he was only trying to protect his closest friend.

Whether or not he should have snooped at my note, he'd seen it, and I understood why it seemed pretty damning from the outside.

My first job once Cameron was okay — and he would be okay — was to put a damn lock on my phone.

I sped along the roads as fast as possible, even though I was certain we'd be waiting a long time before we got an update on Cameron. He looked so helpless trapped in the car, and when he said he had no sensation in his legs...

And yet, he was still his usual upbeat and optimistic self right up until the moment he passed out. I adored his spirit, even though in normal times, it could definitely be a bit much without Hugh around to provide the yin to his yang.

A nagging voice in the back of my head kept reminding me I needed to decide what to do about the TV show, and fast. I'd have to get a flight in about six hours if I didn't want to pass up the opportunity, but the very idea of flying away from Cameron right then made me sick to my stomach.

"Connect my phone to the Bluetooth, will you?"

"Huh?" Hugh looked confused.

"My phone, check the Bluetooth settings—there should be a device called *Camvis*. Connect it, please?"

He picked up my phone, and in a few seconds a beeping sound told me it was connected.

"Camvis, call Alexa."

Flooding on the road meant I'd had to slow the car down, which was perfect because I didn't want to risk another accident while trying to talk Alexa down from the roof, which she was about to hit.

"Alexa, Alexa Associates," my agent answered briskly.

"Hey, it's me. I'm sorry for calling so late."

"It's not that late here, Muri. Time difference, remember?"

I rolled my eyes at myself and caught Hugh trying to suppress a smirk. "Yeah, sorry, it's been a long day. I'm not going to make it to dinner tomorrow."

"What?" Alexa screeched, and Hugh leaped on the car controls to turn the volume down.

"Something's come up, and it's really important. Can you can delay it?"

"I don't, Muriel, no. Do you have any idea how many options these people have? How many girls would meet them at a moment's notice for half a chance at what you're being offered?"

I cringed. "I do have a pretty good idea. But there's been an accident, and it might be really serious. I really can't make it."

"I don't know what to s—"

"If you want a shot at ten percent of my fee, you'll call them now and explain," I said firmly, remembering that Alexa worked for me and not the other way around.

A heavy sigh on the other end of the line told me I'd won this round. "Fine, I'll try. But no promises. I hope whoever's been hurt is okay, and just know that if you're lying to me, I will find you, and I will kill you."

I laughed ruefully. "I wish it was a lie, Alexa, I really do. Keep me informed about how it goes. See ya."

When the call ended, Hugh looked over me, appearing impressed despite himself. "Thanks for doing that. Cameron would appreciate it."

"I can't leave him," I said simply, and for a while we continued to drive in a slightly less awkward silence than before.

"Say," Hugh said with a note of curiosity in his voice, and I braced myself for more questions about my list. "What's your car's name again?"

Oh, God. I flushed scarlet and gave a quick prayer for a sinkhole to appear for me to fall into it and die. Nothing happened, so I was forced to answer.

"Er, the car's a rental, it doesn't have a name," I said, hoping to God that he'd buy it.

"I don't think so," he said, now failing to contain his chuckling. "That device you wanted to connect to. That App."

"Oh, fine. It's Camvis, okay?"

"Cam and Davis, huh? It's better than okay, it's amazing." He openly laughed at me. "Although I might have suggested HughM—"

"Shut up," I snapped, and he did as he was told. For a moment.

"So, Davis and Moore had a ring to it. Or, for a play on words, what about More of Davis? Davis is morish?" He chuckled to himself.

I started tapping the steering wheel in frustration.

"You really did miss us while you were living the high life in LA? Given you named your voice-activated phone servant after us. Most people stick with Siri."

"Of course I missed you. I said I did. And I'd miss you even *more* if I went back, now I've had a taste of exactly what I'll be missing." I raised an eyebrow at Hugh. "I do want *more* of the same."

Hugh flushed slightly as we both remembered how amazing our time together had been. "But you didn't cancel the meeting with the TV folks. You only delayed it."

That was a heavily loaded statement, and it stung. "I'm doing what I can, Hugh. I need time to work things through in my own mind, and I'm not getting any. Whatever happens, I'm going to be making massive life-changing decisions. I need time."

"I get it. I can only think properly when I'm alone, too. But I just don't understand how there's any contest between some dumb show and us."

"I wouldn't expect you to understand. But honestly, that is not the sum total of the dilemma."

It was true; I didn't think Hugh could comprehend having a disconnect between his head and his heart. He seemed so certain of right and wrong. I was messier than that, I guess. "But for what it's worth, the idea of staying here is very appealing. I just hope that Cameron is okay."

"You and me both," he said as we pulled into the hospital parking lot.

We practically ran into reception and asked about Cameron at the desk.

"Are you family?"

"Yes. I'm his brother," Hugh snapped back without any hesitation. Proving even my honest reporter can lie when motivated to.

"He's in surgery," the receptionist told us. "Please, have a seat, and we'll let you know as soon as we have any information."

We took a pair of hard plastic seats in the waiting room, and I bit my nails down to the quick.

Hugh took to tapping out tunes with his feet until I grabbed his leg and stopped him.

I wanted to talk, to explain my reasoning behind every bullet point on my list, and find out if he had any ideas for how I might possibly get everything I wanted. If anyone could solve my problem it would be logical, methodical Hugh. But he was still too angry; I sensed I needed to let it lie for now.

Someone sat opposite us. When I looked up all the heat was sucked from the room and I shivered. Elijah.

"Hugh."

"Eli."

"Muriel."

"Hm." I turned my nose up at him. Childish, yes, but I was too tired and too pissed off with the world to be mature right now.

"What you here for?"

Hugh and I both hesitated, and I decided to let him take the lead. "Cameron's been in a bad accident. He's in surgery. We're waiting to find out how he is. You?"

"Wife's stubbed her toe, dumb bitch."

I recoiled at his heartless words.

"What?" he said, looking pointedly at me. "You think getting blind drunk and walking barefoot into a table isn't dumb?"

"She's married to you, so I'd say being blind drunk twenty-four seven is very wise," I said, and Hugh laughed openly.

"You still bitter that I caught you cheating on your homework after all these years?" he asked, leaning forward and resting his hands on his knees in an almost intimidating stance.

"I wasn't cheating," I pointed out, not that I cared what he thought. "And no. I happen to think you're a jackass, is all."

He leaned back, wagging his finger and giving us both a menacing grin. "Oh, I know. Hughy-boy and Cameron have told you about the little 'conversation' we had when they were dating Hannah, haven't they?"

I shrugged. "Yes."

"And I bet I know why." He continued, leering at me. "You three were always hanging out together at school. I should have guessed their history of sick threesomes went back further."

My face burned red, and Hugh tried to give my back a subtle reassuring squeeze, but Eli's beady little eyes noticed, and he cackled.

"Aw, man. Muriel, I thought you were better than this."

I sensed Hugh was too exhausted to fight back.

"What business is it of yours?" I demanded.

"What y'all get up to is an abomination," Eli replied. "It reflects badly on the whole town when... deviants like you roam the streets. I'm a councilman, so unlike you, I actually care about this place."

"Oh yeah?" Hugh said, roaring into life. "So how come houses out there have been destroyed because the flood defenses were so poor? How come it takes me writing an article to get the fire department basic equipment? And how come the block around Jubilee Street has been zoned for residential when the soil toxicity readings were off the scale? If you care so much, what are you doing about important stuff?"

Fired up at seeing Eli momentarily lost for words, I had to join in. "Yeah, and how come your shirt clashes with your pants?"

Okay, that wasn't *quite* as good as Hugh's, but I made Eli look down at himself uncertainly, so I took it as a win.

"You know, I see your mom around a lot, Muriel," Eli said, suspiciously calm. "She and I tend to have lunch at the same places."

"Because you're a middle-aged mom?" I suggested to Hugh's delighted guffaw.

"Because, unlike you, she has good taste," Eli retorted.

I started to wonder whether this was a meandering set-up to a 'your mom' joke.

"I'll have to tell her I saw you tonight with one of your boyfriends, waiting around for the other one."

Yesterday, there would have been no greater threat possible. But right now, with everything that was happening, it didn't even bother me for a second.

"Well, bless your heart, you go on ahead. Although she'll probably wonder why one of our councilmen has time to spread pathetic gossip."

Before Eli had a chance to answer, Hugh raised a hand. "Look, Cameron might be dying right now. For once in your life, can you be a little bit considerate and leave us alone?"

The door from one of the treatment rooms opened and an attractive young woman hobbled out toward us. She was the very epitome of a Georgia peach girl, all blonde hair and healthy tan, and my jaw almost hit the floor when she sidled up beside Eli and it became clear she was his wife.

"Hey, Hugh," she said, giving a flirty little wave that had me raising an eyebrow.

"Hey, Rita. I heard you stubbed your toe?"

"I dropped a hammer on it," she explained, and we both winced. "Yeah, I was doing some storm clean up, and this genius here decided to prank me by jumping out of a cupboard."

"Clever," I said.

Eli's face turned sheepish as he was caught out on the lie.

"A woman who can do repairs? Hold on to this one, Eli," Hugh said mischievously.

"He ain't got a choice; he's hopeless without me. Well, we'd better go. Bye, Hugh."

She gave that same finger-wiggling wave again, and Eli quickly ushered her out of the building.

"So that's why he hates you so much."

"Because of the three-way thing? Yeah, I told you that."

"No. Can't you see? His wife has a huge crush on you."

Hugh's face screwed up with doubt. "No, she doesn't. She works at the paper, so she recognizes me, that's all."

"Trust you not to be able to see the most obvious crush in history. Elijah's jealous. That's why he gives you a hard time. I only have to hope there's no reason for me to be jealous too."

"Please," he said, shaking his head. "How many times do we have to tell you there's nobody for us except you? If you'll have us."

"I'm teasing," I reassured him. "It is kind of good to learn he's probably not really that interested in your relationships, though. Perhaps nobody in this town cares."

"I don't think they do."

Our little run-in with Elijah provided a good distraction, but we were soon back to indulging in our nervous habits as we waited for news about Cameron. Finally, we took turns to nap, sprawling uncomfortably on the chairs with our jackets draped as blankets over us.

Eventually, the double doors at the back of the waiting room swung open, and we turned to see a surgeon heading toward us.

"You're here for news about Cameron Moore, yes?"

We nodded.

"He's stable. We've done what we can to save his legs, but I'm afraid it's still touch and go. We're going to observe him over the next couple of days, but at this moment in time, amputation can't be ruled out."

It was half expected, but I still gasped at hearing the words.

The terrible news hit me like a hurricane.

Hugh and I had to steady each other as we tried to process it. Cameron, the active, fun-loving cop, might lose his legs? It didn't bear thinking about, and I hated the thought of him sitting in his recovery room alone.

"Can I see him now?" I asked.

The doctor shook his head. "He's conscious, and remarkably lively, but it's family only, and I understand his father is on his way here now."

No. I had to see him.

"I'm his fiancée, doesn't that count as family?"

At exactly the same time as Hugh said, "I'm his brother, practically."

The doctor's face brightened as he looked between us. "Ah. A fiancée and a brother. I didn't realize, so you may come this way."

I tried not to look guilty as I declared, "And Hugh's my fiancé, too."

"Err, excuse me?"

I looked up at Hugh for reassurance and practically saw him say to himself *fuck it*, when he decided to go along with my story. "Yeah, we know it's unusual, but we are all basically family, so we'd really like to see Cameron if at all possible, and he'd definitely want to see us too."

The doctor glanced over at the receptionist, who was clearly fascinated by the exchange.

I didn't feel embarrassed at all; why would I be ashamed of love? The receptionist gave a shrug and a nod to the surgeon, who gave us one last glance before ushering us down the hall.

"You know, I watched a documentary about a relationship like yours a while ago," he said good-naturedly as we walked. "I have to say, they seemed very happy. Nice to have an extra person to split the bills with, too."

"That's a benefit I hadn't thought of," I replied.

Hugh just smirked.

Chapter Eighteen
Cameron Moore

"Oh, why don't you come on over, Muuuuriielll."

She looked dazzling as she entered my little hospital room, and her look of joy—or was it confusion? No, surely joy—as I serenaded her only made her more beautiful. Morphine was a wonderful thing.

Hugh followed in behind her. He looked so pleased to see me I almost wanted to cry. I felt so lucky to have two awesome people caring about me.

"Um, thanks for the song." Muriel sat gently on the end of the bed. "How are you?"

"You deserve it. And I feel... okay. I'm alive, which is good, and you're here, which is even better."

Muriel laughed. "I don't think my presence is better than you being alive, Cameron."

"I strongly disagree."

A shadow of sadness crossed her face, but that might have been the drugs making me paranoid.

"What have they told you about the surgery?" Hugh asked. He'd taken a seat right beside me, and he was looking at me with concern. I swallowed hard.

"They said it went as well as can be expected," I explained. "But there's a lot of physical therapy in my future, at least. And there's a possibility that—" I choked. I couldn't say it. Hugh reached out and touched my arm lightly.

"We know."

"Nothing's definite, though," Muriel said. "And a certain someone told me today that miracles happen all the time, so..."

She looked over at Hugh, and I turned in surprise.

"Have you been taking hippy pills, Hugh? That doesn't sound like you."

He chuckled. "It's been a very strange day, that's for sure."

Muriel accidentally brushed my leg with her arm, but I only knew that because I was looking at her at the time. I didn't feel a thing. My heart sunk, and tears pricked at my eyes.

"What'll I do if I lose my legs? I can't be a cop anymore, and I don't want to do anything else."

"It's not going to happen," Hugh said. Normally, when he said something positive, I believed it, because he'd never knowingly looked on the bright side of life before.

But if he'd been talking about miracles, I was suddenly uncertain about trusting his judgment. That was the kind of crap I normally said, not him. I wondered what sort of magic Muriel had been weaving on him all day.

"Doctors have to tell you the worst-case scenario, in case you sue them."

"Maybe," I said, unconvinced. Somehow, even through the haze of drugs, I didn't seem able to find any optimism in my situation. "Hey, it seems like we've somehow body-swapped. You're Mr. Positive, and I'm the dour cynic."

Hugh laughed, handing me a sandwich from his bag. I took it readily; I hated hospital food. "It's a lot easier to be positive when you're not the one laid up, remember."

"Exactly," Muriel said. "And here's something that'll cheer you up. We're engaged."

"Er, what?" I said, looking between them both in surprise. "I don't remember popping the question... are these drugs really that strong?"

"You're *fake* engaged." Hugh jumped in before Muriel said anything more. "And so am I, apparently. But I'm also your brother. It's the only way we could get in here to see you, because only relatives are allowed in."

"Ahh," That made sense, although I couldn't help feeling a little deflated that I hadn't really come around after surgery to find I had a wedding to plan with Muriel.

"Yes, but—" Muriel began, but Hugh made a clicking noise with his tongue that stopped her for a moment. A cloud of anger shrouded her face until she shook it away and continued, a little louder this time. "Yes, but I do want to say that I love you. I love you so much I can't imagine my life without you. I'm so annoyed at the time we've lost between high school and now, and I don't want to waste another second."

I was speechless.

She'd been running so hot and cold with us that I'd considered it a huge success that I'd convinced her to have dinner at my place. Now she was declaring her love? It seemed that Hugh had been dabbling in magic of his own, the surly little charmer.

"I... I love you too."

Muriel ran around the bed to hug me. Our lips met, and I took hers greedily, grateful to still be able to feel that, at least. She grabbed my face between her hands and held on with a drowning grip as our tongues explored each other, and I took in her comforting scent.

When we reluctantly pulled away, I turned to see Hugh looking completely unmoved.

"What's wrong?" I asked. "Aren't you happy?"

The long pause before he answered told me everything I needed to know. "Yeah, sure I'm happy," he said finally, adjusting his face to a smile with obvious effort. "It's taken Muriel a while, but I'm glad she's settled on what she wants."

Did I detect sarcasm in his voice? No, surely not. This was the best news I'd had since I got on the force, and I felt like I could float out of bed with Muriel in my arms.

"I *have* settled on what I want," Muriel replied, again possibly with a little bite in her tone. "And I'm so sorry I wasn't quick enough for some people. It wasn't easy."

"We know it wasn't. And completely understand that." I patted her hand reassuringly. "But you're here now, and that's all that matters."

"Here for now," Hugh muttered.

"All this sarcasm and muttering is too stressful. Has something happened today?"

Muriel and Hugh both tried to answer at the same time, but they were interrupted by a nurse poking her head around the door.

"Cameron, your dad's here. If your current visitors can say their goodbyes, I'll bring him through."

"Okay, thanks," I said, but Hugh asked the nurse whether he could stay for one more minute.

She agreed.

"I'll see you outside," Hugh said to Muriel, and she glared at him. I'd never been so confused in my life.

With a large sigh and a promise to come back later, Muriel left. As soon as the door clicked shut, I turned to Hugh.

"Right, tell me what's going on?" I demanded, having had enough of being out of the loop.

"She's only saying those things because she's been worrying about you. Understandable given this." He waved his hand at me in the hospital bed.

"That's what this is about? Look, buddy, I love you, but I'm not going to let your pessimism ruin things. You heard what she just said. This is too important."

Hugh didn't respond at first. He just sat back in his chair with his head in his hands. "She's been offered a job."

"What kind of job?"

"A big job. A good job. In LA."

"Oh." I considered this news for a moment. "But long distance isn't so bad, is it? How long is the flight time, a few hours? We can make it work."

"Nope, we can't. She's going to be on a TV show, high profile. If she's going to be famous, she doesn't want it getting out that she's in an unconventional three-way relationship. So it's over, Cameron, no matter what she just said."

"Wow." It was a lot to take in, and I couldn't make sense of it all so quickly.

Hugh nodded.

"You know, when the doctor told me that I might never walk again, I really thought that was going to be as bad as my day was going to get. I thought, *well, Cameron, the only way is up now*, but here we are."

"Here we are," Hugh repeated. "I'm sorry I told you, but I thought the longer I waited, the harder it would be."

"Get her back in here."

"But your dad's waiting. He'll be dying to see you."

"He can wait five more minutes. We need to talk," I demanded.

I needed to talk to my girlfriend or whatever Muriel was.

My head was spinning, and not just from the drugs.

Why would Muriel tell me she loved me—loved us—and that she wanted to be with us forever, when she knew she was leaving? She wasn't a liar. There must have been a misunderstanding, or Hugh was being his old cynical self, or something. There was no way Muriel would let us down like that.

While I waited for them to return, I tentatively reached down to touch my legs. To my delight, I sensed something when I prodded them; not pain, exactly, but a pins and needles sensation that hadn't been there before.

I leaned back against my pillows, and I'd just started drifting off again when Hugh came back in the room with Muriel. Their faces were grim.

"We can do this another time," Hugh offered. "You look like you need sleep."

I waved the offer away. "If I sleep now, I'll only dream of Muriel dumping us to be on The Bachelor." It pleased me to see their serious expressions soften ever so slightly.

"I'm so sorry, Cameron," Muriel started. "I—"

"Just tell us the truth, Muri," I said. "We're big boys. We can take it."

"What we can't take is the constant flip-flopping." Hugh joined in, and I glared at him for his harsh tone. He sighed and adopted a calmer manner. "You've wavered between staying and going, loving us and not wanting to have anything to do with us, a dozen times since last night. It isn't fair."

Muriel's face reddened, and she appeared to bite her tongue in an attempt to hold back. What? I didn't know. But seeing her chastised, I wanted to reach out and comfort her, but Hugh was right. She'd done more U-turns than Vic did without his GPS, and I hadn't even been with them most of the day.

"So, what's this job Hugh told me about?" I asked, hoping to get the conversation flowing again.

"It's a reality series," Muriel started.

"Like Keeping Up with the Kardashians?" I asked, and she grinned.

"I knew you'd know the kind of show I'm talking about. Yeah, so cameras would follow me around, and I'd just... live my life, I guess."

"And she'd get two hundred thousand dollars for it," Hugh added.

Muriel glared across at him. "It's not about that. Not that the money wouldn't be nice, but it's not my main consideration."

"Two hundred grand would be more than nice." I said.

Hugh slouched moodily on the seat as if money shouldn't figure in any deliberations.

"Dude, that's a house. She could buy a whole house at twenty-three. We can't deny her that."

"It's not about the money, guys. If I did the show, I'd have to live in LA, and two hundred does *not* buy you a house there unless you want to live in a parking garage. It's more of a long-term career thing; it would be good to launch my fashion designs."

"I totally get it," I said, and it was true.

Would it kill me to lose Muriel again? Yes, of course, it would. Given the choice, I wouldn't want to let her out of my sight for the rest of my life, but it was not my choice to make — it was hers. And it was also her choice whether to go public with any relationship, let alone a three-way one that would naturally raise eyebrows and maybe damage her brand before it even got off the ground.

"I'm sorry I told you I loved you. I've just been so worried about you. I got carried away. I mean, it's true, of course, but I should have waited until I was certain of my plans before getting your hopes up."

"My hopes are always up. It's how I live, so don't worry, it's fine."

"So, you're doing the show then?" Hugh demanded, breaking the conciliatory mood I'd managed to create. "You're acting like you still don't know, but you have to know by now."

"I honestly don't." Muriel's voice was rough with frustration and tiredness. "I don't even know if y'all would have me now that I've messed you around so much."

"Good point. We're done with you, Muriel, we never liked you anyway," I said, and the smirk on her face told me that my sarcasm had reached my tone. "Why don't you sleep on it? Take your time and come back whenever you're ready."

She nodded and stood to leave. Before heading for the door, she reached down and gave me another kiss; this one sweet and tender, and she pulled away with a sad smile.

"I hope you rest well," she said, and I waved my hands in the air.

"Hey, I forgot. I've got some sensation back in my legs. When you two were out there arguing, I started poking at my legs, and I got pins and needles back."

"That's great." Hugh squeezed my shoulder with his strong hand. "Let's hope you keep improving, and I'll be meeting you in a bar tomorrow night to shoot the shit."

I noticed that he'd pointedly left Muriel out of his imaginary scene, and she obviously noticed too, as her eyes grew wide with hurt.

"Right, get some rest. See you tomorrow," Hugh said, and they both left.

I pressed the buzzer to call the nurse and tell them my dad could come in, and also to inform them about the sensation in my legs.

Aside from Hugh, my dad was the smartest person alive. He'd have some good advice for me. Pessimism wasn't going to defeat us, I decided. Everything was going to work out for the best.

Chapter Nineteen
Hugh Davis

I left Cameron's room feeling no less dejected than I had before.

How could Muriel let things get out of hand, saying that she loved us and didn't want to waste another second apart from us?

I started walking away with the intention of calling a cab, Muriel had driven me around enough for one day, and we both needed space. But she gripped my forearm and dragged me into an empty treatment room, closing the door behind us.

"Why the hell did you tell him that I might be leaving?" Muriel demanded, looking like she was ready to kill me with her bare hands. "Don't you think he's got enough to deal with right now?"

"I had to. You were telling him you wanted to be with us, and I know Cameron. He would've sat in that hospital bed picking out a suit to wear for our wedding, and the next thing he'd know, you'd be gone forever."

Muriel jumped up on the exam table and sat with her arms folded. "You were wrong to tell him tonight, right after his surgery. And you know it."

Was I wrong?

Deep down, I knew I was.

Just as Muriel had said she wouldn't promise Cameron the world, I said I wouldn't crush his world. Perhaps a little bit of hope was exactly what Cameron needed to get him through the night, and because of my pride and obsession with being right, I'd destroyed that. We'd both let our friend down.

I looked at Muriel and uttered the words I always hated saying. "You're right; I was wrong."

"Okay, that wasn't so hard, was it?" she replied, not knowing exactly how difficult it was for me to admit I was fallible. "Now, what are we going to do?"

"What Cameron said, I guess. Go home and sleep. And you have a certain list to finish writing—"

"Do you think, maybe, you could talk through my options with me in the morning?" Muriel nodded her head in the direction of Cameron's room. "Despite getting things so spectacularly wrong in there, I have to admit you're a smart guy. Perhaps there are details I'm not including in my deliberations or a solution I'm not seeing?"

I shook my head sadly. "What Cameron said is true. This is your choice, and yours alone. All I would ever do is ask you to stay."

"Perhaps that's the advice I want to hear," she said quietly, and I turned away from her pleading eyes.

The harsh fluorescent light above our heads flickered, making it seem like we were in a horror film; the perfect atmosphere for my current mood.

Muriel seemed to be drowning in indecision, and I still couldn't understand why it was such a difficult decision to make.

Cameron seemed to understand, which surprised me given that losing her would hit him even harder it would me, and—

I gasped as a solution came to me in an instant. It would get us ninety percent of what we wanted, but that was a whole lot better than zero, so it was worth a shot.

"I've got it. I think. I know how this can work."

Muriel took hold of my jacket sleeves and pulled me to her. She looked up at me with hope in her beautiful eyes, and my heart twisted in pain.

"I had every confidence you'd figure it out. Come on then, my big sexy genius."

After a moment's hesitation, I made an offer I never thought I'd have to make. "You should date Cameron. Just Cameron. I'll step aside. It'll hurt, but I'll survive, and you two can go on TV and be all cute together."

Silence.

Muriel's face slowly changed from excited to confused and finally furious. She pushed me away from her. "How dare you, Hugh? How fucking dare you."

"What?" I was genuinely confused by her reaction to my genius idea. "You can never get everything in life, but this is a compromise that gets you and Cameron almost everything."

"Do you seriously believe that if you weren't an enormous part of what I want, I wouldn't have thought of that already? Do you think I'm a total idiot?"

I stuttered. "No, I just, I—"

"You think I'm playing at this, don't you? You never considered I might really commit to you both. Admit it, you've doubted me from the start."

That wasn't true.

Or was it?

What about when we were at the bungalow, in our little bubble where reality didn't exist? Even then, I was wracked with uncertainty, and only when we were having sex did I believe everything was going to be all right. I'd hidden my doubts pretty well, but it seemed she read me like a book.

On the other hand—

"Do you blame me?" I argued back. "You're the flakiest person I've ever met. You ran away from us all those years ago, and okay we were all young then, but from the start it was obvious you'd do the same again."

Muriel snorted with derision, but I wasn't ready to stop.

"And you told Cameron you love him before me."

"I love you both," proclaimed an exasperated Muriel.

I held a hand up to stop her. "You didn't say that. I'm not even mad. This just makes sense. You've got more in common with Cameron, and his happiness means the world to me, so I'm going to let you two get on with it."

Muriel jumped down from the bed and stood in front of me, her eyes bright with tears.

"I know what this is about. You don't respect me because of what I do."

"What? That's bullshit; I've never said a bad word about your job."

"You don't have to say anything. It's clear in your body language."

"Oh, you're a body language expert now, are you?"

Muriel slammed her hand down on the bed, and I had to admit I was surprised at the strength of her anger.

"Whenever I mention my work; my photoshoots, my followers, when my mom talked about the ads I was in. Every single time you look disgusted like we're talking about cleaning toilets."

"At least cleaning toilets has a purpose." I instantly regretted saying that, it came out all wrong.

She gazed up at me, and any hint of affection or respect she had for me was gone from her eyes.

"Hugh Davis, I always mistook you for a charming, brooding pessimist. But, it turns out, you're just an asshole."

She walked out, leaving me standing alone with my mouth hanging open.

It seemed I managed to come up with the worst idea in the world, *and* I mortally offended her because I chose a quick quip over actually discussing my feelings.

Good job, Hugh. Great work.

I smacked my forehead with the palm of my hand. *Why are you the way you are?*

After a few minutes spent lamenting all the things I should have done differently to avoid being called an asshole, like not behaving like an asshole, I walked back out into the reception to call a cab home. On my way, I bumped into Butch, Cameron's dad, who had just left his son's bedside.

I must have looked terrible because, despite everything that must have been on his mind, when he caught sight of me, he tilted his head in concern.

"Hugh, you okay, buddy?"

I heaved a sigh. "I'm fine, thanks, Mr. Moore."

"You certainly don't look it."

I tried to wave away his concern.

"No, seriously. You look like crap warmed up. Cameron's going to be fine. He's getting more sensation back in his legs by the minute. He's pretty much out of danger."

A bit of good news, at last. I smiled and thanked him for sharing the good news, but before I could head off, he took hold of my shoulder and looked me in the eye.

"That's not what's troubling you, is it?"

I shrugged and tried again to walk away. Butch didn't need to listen to anyone else's problems right then. Like his son, he had a heart of diamond-studded gold, so he refused to be brushed aside.

"Come on, my boy, let's sit down. Remember how you used to call me Fake Dad when your real dad couldn't help you out as much as he wanted to?"

I smiled at the memory.

My dad worked such long hours when I was a kid that he was rarely around to play ball or tell me about girls, and my mom's only advice was that girls break hearts and I should keep my head in my books.

Butch was friends with my dad, and he agreed to take me under his wing.

He ended up giving me advice on every subject from trigonometry to the birds and bees. I wouldn't have achieved my dream of becoming a journalist without his guidance.

"I remember. I don't think I ever thanked you properly for that."

"Don't you dare thank me. It was a joy to help you, and I'm getting the feeling you need a bit more of that fake dad advice now."

I simply nodded and let Butch guide me over to some seats in the almost empty waiting room.

"Now, let's get us some hot cocoa."

I moved to object, but he held a finger up to stop me.

"Don't even try to tell me you're too good for hospital cocoa. I was in here last year with a hernia, and this stuff is the only thing that kept me going. Well, that and the company of Ms. Terrance over there." He nodded in the direction of the receptionist behind the desk, who rolled her eyes but also blushed with a smile.

I shook my head and chuckled. These Moore men, if they bottled their charm and sold it, they'd be millionaires.

Butch soon returned with a couple of steaming hot styrofoam cups. I placed mine on the floor to let it cool while Butch took a long sip of his, smacking his lips in satisfaction when he was done.

"That's the stuff. Now, what's going on with you?"

"It's nothing. It's just... my love life is complicated at the moment."

Butch nodded. "Muriel?"

I blinked in surprise. "Well, yeah. How did you know?"

"I was just talking to Cameron. Do you seriously think he'd keep something like that to himself? He's been giddy about the idea of Muriel moving back since the day she left."

I grabbed my cocoa and took a slurp. It was still too hot, but I needed a pause to process what I was hearing. "So... you know, then?"

"Know what?" Butch said innocently.

"Don't mess with me." I waggled my finger at him in a mock-scold. "Do you know what I think you know? The thing most parents don't know about their children?"

"That y'all have shared girlfriends before? Sure, like I said, he tells me everything."

"Oh."

"Yup. I got to hear all about Hannah; boy, she was a piece of work."

I nodded in agreement. "Yeah, not our finest hour."

"Muriel's different, isn't she? You two were always crazy about her from the first day you met."

"She's different all right."

We sat in silence for a minute, drinking our cocoa and watching the hospital staff go about their work.

"I've fucked it up, Butch. Excuse my language."

"You're excused. You're a grown man now." Butch chuckled. "And I'm sure you haven't fucked it up."

I wasn't ready to laugh about the situation. I leaned forward and rested my head in my hands until Butch's hand press comfortingly on my back.

"Let's go for a walk."

We got up and headed out of the hospital.

It was the first time I'd taken fresh air into my lungs in hours. I breathed deeply a few times, savoring the calming sensation and enjoying the slight coolness in the early morning air.

We sauntered down a couple of blocks before we spoke again.

"So, you were saying you've messed things up with Muriel. I'll bet you haven't, not really."

"I said her job was less noble than toilet-cleaning," I said dejectedly, embarrassed by my actions but determined not to pretend I was any better a person than I was.

"Ah. Well, that wasn't clever, was it?"

"Nope. And I don't even believe it. I don't love her job, but I don't have to—just like she doesn't love the minutia of local politics. I like her passion, no matter what it's for."

That, and she'd seemed really interested in starting to use her profile to highlight good causes. I'd hoped to help her with it, and we'd work together on campaigns. But even if she did nothing but advertise lip-gloss for the rest of her life, I'd still love her with every beat of my heart.

"Can I ask you something personal?" Butch asked, and I eyed him suspiciously.

"You already know plenty of pretty personal stuff about me, it turns out, so yeah, why not."

"Do you think you wanted to torpedo this relationship, deep down?"

"Um, nope," I said, suddenly doubting my decision to confide in Butch. Why the hell would I sabotage the best thing that ever happened to me? "That makes literally no sense, I'm afraid."

A group of women walked toward us, obviously heading back from a night out at a club. They were singing and dancing down the street, and we had to dodge out of their way to avoid getting dragged into their little street party. One of them dropped a plastic cup, and I stopped to pick it up, dropping it in the trash can nearby.

"You're a good man. But seriously. I'm no psychologist, so this is only a hunch here, but by any chance, could you have been hoping the relationship would fail so you wouldn't have to... I don't know... face telling your mother about it?"

Before I objected, he quickly added, "Subconsciously, I mean. Deep down. I mean, you did compare her life's work to toilet maintenance."

"I accused her of preferring Cameron, too," I groaned. This time, Butch didn't say anything, he just pulled an expression that was a combination of sympathy and cringe.

A neon OPEN sign flashed up ahead, indicating a 24/7 liquor store was back in business after the storm. The windows were mostly boarded up, and sandbags lined the front, but otherwise, it was business as usual.

Businesses that were so resilient that they got back up on their feet as though nothing had happened always impressed me.

At that moment, I was also very tempted to support the local store by buying and drinking a fifth of rum, but I thought better of it; perhaps some gum would be good.

"She doesn't prefer Cameron," Butch said reassuringly. "Or at least, she didn't until the toilet comment." He shook his head, almost certainly marveling at the mess I'd gotten myself into.

Butch waited on the sidewalk while I went in and bought gum at the liquor store. While I waited in line behind the customers, I mulled over what Butch had said.

Could it be true? I loved my mom more than anyone else in the world, but was it possible I was scared of her? I'd faced down bulldog lawyers and seedy landlords alike in my job, so it hardly seemed logical that a diminutive middle-aged woman frightened me, but then the lawyers didn't have the power of holding passive-aggressive guilt trips over me.

I recalled what my mom had said.

Muriel preferred Cameron. She always had, and I'd been a third-wheel this whole time. I'd wanted to argue with her, but I'd have had to admit there was something going on between the three of us. So I'd simply walked away. But if we did end up in a real relationship, I'd have no choice but to tell her; if I didn't, the grapevine would.

Shit, Bruce was right.

"Dr. Phil, eat your heart out," I said as I rejoined Butch in the street, and we started our trek back to the hospital. "You may have a point about my mom."

"I don't blame you. Your mom is terrifying."

My head swiveled to face him, my brain automatically going into defense mode at the mention of my mom, and Butch put his hands up innocently. "I like her, don't get me wrong. But she's always been fiercely protective of you, with emphasis on the fierce."

"Muriel's fierce too," I said dreamily. "And fiery. I love that about her."

"Well, one word of advice; don't tell any woman she reminds you of your mother. She won't like it. And, frankly, it's a bit weird."

"I'll be lucky to even get a chance to speak to Muriel again. But if there's even a glimmer of hope, I won't blow it a second time. I gotta put an end to the mama's boy thing, anyway. Doesn't really go with the whole hard boiled investigator vibe I'm going for."

Butch laughed. "Yeah, that's a weird combination for sure. Anyway, I'm sure you'll be fine. When you do make up with Muriel, be sure to drop in on Cameron again; it sounds like he's got an idea or two up his sleeve."

"Hasn't he always?" I replied.

Butch tapped his nose conspiratorially, refusing to say anything more.

We said our goodbyes, and I called a cab home, with a tiny ray of hope that I might sort things out with Muriel before she left for good.

Chapter Twenty
Muriel Tennyson

I stepped out of the hospital into the cool night air and took a deep breath. *Breathe in for four, hold for four. Breathe out for four, hold for four.* That was what my yoga teacher had taught us as a foolproof method of relaxing. Well, bullshit, I'd tell her if I ever saw her again. I needed more than mere oxygen to calm my nerves. I needed a punching bag, or a stiff drink, or a... *a good fuck.*

Geez Louise, Muriel, I thought as I made my way back to the car. *Even now, after everything that's happened, you still want those men as much as ever?*

I used to be that girl who would fake orgasms to go to sleep quicker, and now my body craved sex from the very man who had me shaking with rage in the middle of the night?

Madness.

I unlocked my car and got inside. Perhaps a drive would help clear my mind. I used my phone to set up a good playlist, full of cheesy hits and one-hit-wonders, partly to cheer me up but also because it would piss Hugh off. Petty, moi?

Having pulled out of the parking lot, I chose a journey that would take me down some long, open roads. Mindless driving, that was what I needed.

For about thirty minutes, I just drove, singing at the top of my voice as Katy Perry, Taylor Swift, and Destiny's Child did their best to cheer me right up. I even attempted a rap when Nicki Minaj started playing, but I soon stopped when I realized it was possible to experience embarrassment even while alone in my car.

With my mind energized, I started to go over the argument I'd had with Hugh.

He was right, I shouldn't have declared my love for either of them before I knew whether we had any kind of future. It was confusing for all of us and liable to break hearts.

My worry for Cameron and the relief of seeing him alive had overwhelmed me, and I'd spoken too soon; I couldn't deny that. But if they wanted me to stay, surely they'd beg me not to go. Even Cameron said I should do what was right for me, when I'd honestly expected him to tell me to stay. Perhaps they didn't care much whether I chose them or left.

Perhaps they weren't as into me as I hoped.

Hugh clearly wasn't; his lack of respect for my job was disappointing, even if I had goaded him into admitting what he really thought.

I lacked a third party: someone to bounce ideas off and bottom this thing out. I checked the time; would Jasmine still be awake?

"Camvis, call Jas," I said, but it went straight to voicemail. I tried Poppy too, but her phone kept ringing without an answer. I was bummed out, but I could hardly blame them for going to sleep.

I wracked my brain trying to come up with anyone else I could call, ideally in LA, so there'd be a chance of them being awake. Of course, there was my agent, but all Alexa would do is tell me to get my hiney on a plane and start making money, so there wasn't any point in trying.

I had a few other friends in California, but they were good-time pals. I wouldn't trust any of them with my problems, especially ones this personal.

Which only left one person.

My mom would probably be awake; she often got insomnia after a storm, and ordinarily, she'd love to pass the long nighttime hours discussing someone's love life. But her own daughter's, when it was a pretty non-traditional love life?

I pulled over at the side of the road to give the matter my full attention. If I didn't pour my issues out to someone tonight, I'd never go to sleep, which meant I wouldn't make a decision in time, and my opportunities with both the boys and the TV show would pass by.

I had no doubt that Hugh was primed and ready to tell Cameron what a bitch I'd been to him, so I needed to act quickly.

"Camvis, call Mom."

"Sweetie? What's wrong? Where are you?"

"I'm fine, Mom," I said, and her relief was palpable even through the phone line. "I'm just driving. It's been a weird day."

"Well, clearly, if you're aimlessly driving around at this hour."

"Exactly. If you're already awake, do you mind if I come over? I want to talk about something with you."

"Sure, hon, come right now. I'll have a cup of hot cocoa ready for you."

"Thanks, Mom."

I dropped the call and swung the car around.

By the time I arrived at my parents' house, I was a nervous wreck. I had imagined a dozen different scenarios where Mom threw me out of the house and promised to never speak to me again. She told me to forget about the boys and go back to LA.

Would that really be such a bad thing for her to say?

The fact that my brain had filed it under 'Nightmare Outcome' definitely said something about my state of mind, but so did the clothing logos I'd been preparing in my head to use after I got famous.

The house was lit up like it was early evening, and I briefly wondered whether they were actually nocturnal.

Locking my car, I headed up the path and knocked on the door shakily. Mom answered in her nightgown, robe, and big fluffy slippers, and she looked so comfortable, I was jealous as hell.

"Sweetie, what's happened?" Her tone was so sympathetic that I collapsed in her arms. I cried, huge gulping sobs, and she stroked my hair tenderly as I let out all of my frustrations.

"You'd better not be staining my nightgown with that mascara of yours." She grinned when my tears had started to subside. I had to laugh since that was pure Mom; at the same time, hugely comforting and completely shallow. Perhaps the apple didn't fall far from the tree after all.

"I'm not wearing any makeup," I promised her.

She took my face in her hands and studied me closely. "Boy trouble. I knew it. Come and get your cocoa."

I followed her through to the living room. "I don't really want cocoa, but thanks anyway."

"You'll want this. Go on, drink it; it's your father's recipe."

With a sigh, I dropped onto the couch and picked up the mug. I took a sip of the warm, chocolatey drink, and my eyes widened with joy. "Whiskey."

"Yup. Figured you could use it."

"I wouldn't say no to a vat of it right now."

She set down her drink and folded her hands in her lap. "Come on; out with it."

It was time. This moment might change my relationship with my family for the rest of my life.

After taking a deep breath, I dove in, explaining how Hugh, Cameron, and I all had feelings for each other. I decided to leave out the more... sensual details and focused on the more romantic side of it. When I was finished, I realized I'd closed my eyes. I opened them slowly, my jaw going slack as I caught my mom sitting there wearing the most satisfied-looking smirk I'd ever seen.

"Mike, you owe me ten bucks," she called to my dad. After a second of no response, she said, "Ah, he can't hear me. He's all the way upstairs."

"What are you talking about?" I asked, utterly bewildered.

"After you were here with Hugh yesterday, I had a bet with your dad," she explained, somewhat sheepishly now that the glow of victory was fading. "I said 'you know what, Mike, I reckon those kids have some kind of menage going on.' There's been a documentary about it."

"So I've heard," I said, still taken aback by her casual acceptance. "And Dad didn't believe it?"

"Nah, he said you were too tough for Cameron, said you'd eat him for breakfast."

I nearly spat out my spiked cocoa at that. "Cameron's tougher than he looks. He's in the hospital right now, actually; his car got hit by a collapsing building. I thought he was going to die, but he's already making great progress."

Mom's expression changed to one of concerned worry. "Is that why you're here? You're worried about him?"

"No. I mean, yes, I'm still worried about him. But I've had a job opportunity, and I don't know what to do about it, and then Hugh and I had a horrible argument and—"

Mom moved to sit beside me on the couch and wrapped her arms around me. "It's okay, sweetie. Calm down and slow down. Tell me about the job."

I explained everything, about the pay and the potential for it to launch my designer career, and about the downsides of fame and the need to live in LA.

As I spoke, the weight lifted off my shoulders. The shame, the guilt, the utter confusion, it was no longer mine to bear alone.

She took everything in and looked incredibly thoughtful. "Well, that is a pickle," she murmured.

I nodded in agreement. "A pickle indeed."

"But there has to be a solution. What it boils down to is, what's your priority? Figure that out, and everything else will fall into place."

I shifted uncomfortably. "Well, there is one other thing. When Hugh and I were fighting about Cameron, it became very clear that he doesn't respect what I do for a living, and he wouldn't respect this TV show."

"I'm sure that's not true."

"Well, it's what he said. He said that toilet cleaning had more purpose than what I do."

Mom shook her head from side to side. "People do need clean toilets—"

I began to object, but she held her hands up in surrender. "That's not what he meant, I know. He said it because he was mad and disappointed that you might be leaving. Now, if he doesn't apologize, I'd give him hell for it, but your dad's a good judge of character and he really thinks highly of Hugh, so I'm certain he'll be kicking himself for saying that to you."

She was right. Hugh wasn't a cruel man; he just had a sharp tongue like me. And I didn't expect him to get excited over a shoe ad or a viral post; frankly, it would be weird if he did.

He *did* get very excited about the photos I took when we were out helping with the clean-up effort, and that was something that actually took skill on my part. Perhaps things were salvageable with him after all.

"So, with that in mind—what's the most important thing to you?"

"Hugh and Cameron," I replied without hesitation. "But... I'm only twenty-three; I have to consider my career too. I want my own life as well, not to just be someone's, or even two people's, arm candy."

My mom beamed with pride. "That's my girl. This is the woman I wanted you to be. Not scared of dating, or scared of sex—" I blushed at her mention of the word, and she shook her head and laughed. "We're both adults now, Muri, I'm sure you don't mind me saying the 's' word anymore. I'm just saying I only ever wanted you to have your own ambitions. It's possible to have it all; you've got to be smart about it."

Those words evaporated any of my remaining tension. Her strict parenting style might not have been what I'd do myself, but knowing that she came from a truly good place meant the world to me.

Unfortunately, it didn't solve my immediate problems.

"I can't see any way of having it all, though. Not when the things I want are diametrically opposed to each other."

"Well," she handed me my drink and leaned toward me conspiratorially. "I have an idea you might like."

Chapter Twenty One
Muriel Tennyson

I needed to speak to Hugh. I dialed his number, and after a few rings, he picked up.

"Ungh?"

"Did I wake you?"

"No, why?"

"You sounded like a caveman when you picked up."

"Dunno, that's just how I answer the phone."

"Well, it's delightful. Can we meet up? I feel bad about our fight earlier; I'm hoping we can talk it out."

"Sure, I feel the same. Wanna go for food and drinks? Let's meet at Smokey Joe's?"

"I have literally no idea what that is, but the name conjures up weird things."

Hugh chuckled quietly. "It's a diner, near the hospital on Rydale Avenue. Maybe we can see if we can visit Cameron too?"

"Okay, sure. See you in one hour?"

I scurried to the bathroom to get a shower and freshen up as best I could, and while the water cascaded over my face, I wondered where I might end up that night. *Go prepared for anything.*

As I wrapped a towel around myself, there was a faint knock at the bathroom door.

"Sweetie? I've left something outside for you. It was going to be for your birthday, but I'll get you something else."

I opened the door and found a fancy shopping bag sitting outside. Inside was a beautiful pink tea dress with a peach print. The Peter Pan collar and smocking down the front made it adorable, but it was short and flippy enough to be quite flirty too. I slipped it over my head and found that it fit like a glove. With extra motivation to look nice, I quickly rummaged around the bathroom and started on my makeup.

The mirror confirmed I actually looked like I'd slept in a bed and not a hospital waiting room chair. Ah, the wonderful power of cosmetics.

The cab honked its horn, I'd decided to leave the rental car behind with my plan of being prepared for anything including Hugh offering to drive me home — his or mine. I ran outside, stopping only to give Mom a huge hug and a kiss of thanks. I couldn't believe how much things had changed between us; I'd gained a best friend. I jumped in the cab and asked him to take me to Smokey Joe's.

"You're a bit well-dressed for that place, if you don't mind me saying, ma'am."

"It's just a standard diner, isn't it?"

"Standard isn't the word I'd use. You've not been there before?"

"No. Why? What's it like?"

"It's like a dive bar, but without the alcohol. The customers usually bring their own."

"Oh. Sounds fun."

It sounded like Hugh. Always seeking whatever urban grime he could get his hands on, I imagined him in there making friends with people from all walks of life and getting the inside story.

I wondered whether they all knew his *best* friend was a cop.

We pulled up outside, and through the steamed-up window I picked out Hugh already in there. I paid the driver and walked through the doors, only to be met by a stench of stale beer and fried food that was so strong I practically had to wade through it.

Even at this early hour, the place was almost full, and a few of them were definitely not sober. *You were drinking whiskey not so long ago*, I reminded myself.

Hugh spotted me from a table on the other side of the diner, and he rose to greet me.

"You look... wow." His eyes widened as I approached. "You look too good for this place. I thought it would be fun to see how I get some of my stories, but not today. Let's go down the road."

"I do not have a problem with that," I said, smiling as he took my hand and led me out of the bizarre diner.

"There's a *Starbucks* down the road. Let's keep it simple, okay?" he asked, and I nodded enthusiastically.

"I'd do terrible things for a coffee with at least two thousand calories in it right now."

Hugh looked down and waggled his eyebrows as we walked down the street. "What kind of things?"

"Hey, less of that, mister," I said in a chastising tone. "I'm not doing anything to a man who insults my job like you did."

His face turned serious, and he pulled open the coffee shop door to allow me inside. "Ah. Yeah, well, let's get our coffee, and we'll talk about that."

I grabbed a booth while Hugh bought the drinks. He brought them over on a tray, along with a couple of lemon poppyseed muffins; my all-time favorite.

We sat in silence while we enjoyed the muffins; it was obvious that we'd both been too long without a proper meal.

I broke the silence by asking if he'd heard from Cameron. Apparently, he'd been texting Hugh all night with regular updates on his injuries, which were looking much better than they had when we first met the doctor.

He'd also been texting ideas for how to make things work between us, from paying a lookalike to act as decoy for me so I could still see the boys while doing the show, to us all moving to a treehouse in the Andes and living off foraged food. He was a creative man, but not many of the ideas were practical.

With the Cameron update out of the way, there wasn't anything left to do except the hardest thing of all: apologize.

"So."

"So."

"I'm sorry I called you an asshole."

Hugh laughed. "Don't be sorry, I was being the king of assholes."

"That's... quite a horrible image."

He laughed harder, and I joined in, relieved that the tension between us was nowhere near as bad as I'd feared. "Yeah, let's not think about that. Really, I am so, so sorry for what I said. I won't excuse myself by claiming I was tired and emotional, but—"

"But you were," I pointed out mildly. "Your best friend almost died and was still in grave danger. You'd spent the day meeting our parents and rescuing people, and I'd gone completely off-script without warning you."

"Still no excuse." He crumpled a muffin wrapper in his hand and looked genuinely contrite. "I said some hurtful things, and what's stupid is that I don't even believe them. I don't want you to date Cameron without me. I'd rather have my teeth removed without anesthetic."

I held my hand out, and he clasped it. "I can't tell you how happy that makes me."

"I was attempting to make a grand gesture, but in truth, I was just scared."

"Of what?"

I listened as he explained his conversation with Butch, and how he realized he was trying to delay having to tell his mom about his preferred alternative private life and about me. He worried that he seemed childish, and I had nothing but sympathy for him; I understood exactly how he felt.

"But if my mom can accept us all with open arms, I bet yours can too," I said. "I really think your mom and I would get along well; we're quite similar in a lot of ways."

"That's what I said to Butch," Hugh said happily. "But he told me to never mention that. Apparently, women don't like being compared to their boyfriend's mother."

Hugh pulled a face, and I hesitated on hearing the word boyfriend, but we looked at each other and silently agreed to let it pass. "I'll make an exception for Mrs. Davis," I said, and he beamed with joy.

"Oh, and about the whole disrespecting your career thing," Hugh said. I tried to wave him away from the subject, but his face turned serious. "No, I need to say this. I respect you so much. And admire you too. You moved to another state on your own—no safety net—and after only a few years, you've been offered your own TV show. I might not understand your world, Muri, but I recognize awesome when I see it. You are awesome, Muriel, and I really respect you for all you've achieved."

I started to tear up, hearing his lovely, sincere words.

Dammit, I remember a time when I swore men wouldn't make me cry. I fanned my eyes as Hugh looked on with a slight grin on his rugged face. I suppose it meant I'd found the right ones.

"Thank you," I said finally. "Really, I appreciate that so much."

"It's nothing but the truth," Hugh said easily. "Anyway, we're getting a bit serious here. Want me to text Cameron and see if we can go visit? Hopefully he'll be loopy on pain meds again."

"Sure, that'd be great. I'll go to the bathroom and fix my face. I can't believe you've made me cry already."

I headed into the ladies' room and used tissue and cool water to try to de-puff my eyes. It kind of worked. Hugh and I had made up, and I had a plan. Life was looking pretty damn good.

Chapter Twenty Two
Muriel Tennyson

When we called the nurse's desk, the head nurse stated Cameron was wide awake, so Hugh and I walked straight over to the hospital.

As we walked, Hugh wrapped his arm around my back, and his touch through the thin fabric of my dress caused little bolts of electricity to shoot through my body. Would that ever stop? Could I ever grow bored of a man as mysterious as Hugh, or as rambunctious as Cameron; or as hot as either of them? Surely it wasn't possible.

We entered the now too familiar waiting room to find Chrissy there getting a coffee from the vending machine.

"Hey." I pulled her into a sympathetic hug. "How are you doing?"

"Oh, you know," Chrissy said, shrugging expansively. "It was just a wedding. We can rearrange. I'll be honest, I was a little hysterical about it when I first found out, but the accident has put things into perspective."

I murmured agreement and offered to buy her the coffee she was about to get. "How's Vic?"

"He's fine. They kept him overnight because he had a concussion, but they're letting him out soon. I'm here to pick him up. How's Cameron?"

"We're here to see him now," I explained, and Hugh came along to join us.

"He says he's doing well. He's out of the danger zone at least, so he's not going to need any amputations."

"Oh, thank God for that." Chrissy hung her head in sympathy. "You worry so much about them as cops anyway, even without weather to deal with, don't you?"

She looked at me as though I were a fellow cop's wife, and I stuttered slightly, not knowing what to say.

"Oh, I know all about y'all, silly. Vic can't keep his yap shut for a minute."

I smiled uneasily, wondering whether this clearly religious woman would be so accepting of them. "I guess not, if he's anything like his partner."

"Exactly," Chrissy said, smiling.

Hugh grinned too, so I guessed it was all okay.

"And the three of you are just adorable. Ever since school, you've been hanging around together. You always had great chemistry, anyone could see that. And now you're grown up and you're all so gorgeous—"

"You're making us blush, Chrissy," Hugh said, putting his hands on my shoulders for support. "Anyway, we'd better get in and see Cameron. I've got some of his favorite candy, so he won't want to be kept waiting."

"I hope you get to leave with Vic soon," I said.

"Me too. Hey, we should all go out sometime, maybe bowling? Unless you have to get back to California soon, Muriel?" She looked at me quizzically.

"I... er, maybe. It's complicated," I said, and she nodded with understanding.

"Well, we'll see then. Keep us updated on Cameron."

After waving, we went up to the desk to inquire about Cameron.

He'd been moved to a different room because his prognosis was much better and he didn't need as much support. We walked along the corridor, and I realized I had butterflies in my stomach at the prospect of seeing him. I squeezed Hugh's hand, and opened the door to Cameron's room.

"Well, if it isn't my two favorite people." Cameron grinned from ear to ear. "And... are they speaking to each other?"

"We definitely are," Hugh said, putting some hot tamales on Cameron's bedside table while I walked over to plant a kiss on the patient's lips.

"Thank God for that. I thought I was going to have to bonk your heads together."

"How are you doing?" I asked.

His expression darkened slightly. "I've been doing well. The sensation in my legs was increasing consistently, but it seems to have stalled. And I've got no movement yet except my big toe. Look."

He pulled the blanket aside and wiggled his toe for us. I didn't think I'd find anything as simple as a moving digit exciting. But my heart swelled in my chest at the sight of the movement—it meant that he was in with a good chance of getting better.

"That's amazing. Don't worry about it stalling," I assured him. "You were never going to get better in twenty-four hours."

"I kind of hoped I would." Cameron shrugged. "I'm so bored stuck in here."

"We'll visit as much as we can," Hugh said, and I agreed.

"So, you aren't going back to LA yet?" Cameron asked, with hope gleaming in his eyes.

"Yes, what have you decided to do?" Hugh asked. "Did your agent manage to rearrange your meeting?"

Truth be told, I had three voicemail messages from Alexa I hadn't checked yet. I took a deep breath, ready to explain the plan my mom had come up with.

"Wait." Cameron placed his finger on my lips to stop me from talking. I giggled against it, and he pulled away, grinning. "Before you say anything, my dad and I came up with a plan so you wouldn't have to do this show, but you would get to do what you really want to do."

"We aren't moving to Peru, Cam," Hugh said, rolling his eyes.

"Not that, that was the morphine talking. No, listen."

We both sat down in some plastic chairs next to the bed and waited for him to speak.

"So, hear me out. You want to be a fashion designer, right?"

"Yes," I said, suddenly very curious about this idea of his.

"Well, I'm no expert, but I guess you can do that anywhere. The internet exists, you know."

Hugh and I laughed at his mock condescension.

"So, I've got a bit of money stashed away from a payout I got last time I was in an accident."

I gave him a sideways look, and he threw his hands in the air.

"It wasn't my fault, either time. I have bad luck, right? Or good luck, I guess, given the compensation. Anyway, I've got this money and nothing to do with it. So, why don't I lease you a studio, down in the arty part of town? With your following, you should get interest right away, and you could sell online as well as in the studio. You're talented, so I should make my investment back in what, a couple of months?"

He clapped his hands together excitedly, but I was speechless.

When I didn't say anything and the joyful, excited expression started to fall from Cameron's face, Hugh looked over at me, concerned. "What he just said... it's a good idea, isn't it?"

"Mhm."

"Don't tell me you're not interested? Because so help me God, Muriel, if you don't—"

"No, no. It's nothing like that. It's just, my mom came up with the exact same idea this morning. Only I'd use the money they'd been saving for my future wedding. She and Dad figured out I was a non-traditional type of person, and I might like to spend the money on something non-traditional instead."

The guys both stared at me with doubtful expressions. "I'm serious, guys. I've got the money to start my own business."

"Holy shit. That means I can spend the compensation money on a BMW after all."

Hugh and I laughed at him, and Hugh gathered me into a tight, squeezy hug. He kissed the top of my head and whispered, "I'm so happy."

"I'm happy too. I haven't broken the news to my agent yet, but—"

"Do it. Do it. Do it," Cameron cheered, and in a total departure from his usual character, Hugh joined it, obviously giddy from the news.

"All right. It's too early over there yet; I'll call her soon. I'm hoping she won't be too pissed off. I might need her to get contacts. Jasmine and Poppy know people in the business too, so I should be off to a good start."

The door opened, and Cameron's dad popped his head around the door. "Mind if I come in?"

"Get yourself in here, Fake Dad." Hugh stood to give Butch a hearty handshake. "It's a celebration."

"It's an old joke," Butch explained, correctly reading my confused expression.

"Well, the celebration is both for my new business and Cameron's big toe," I replied.

Butch gave his son a hug and sat on the edge of the bed. "Ah, so you're going ahead with our idea?"

"Almost. Only, my parents are putting the money in."

"Perfect," Butch said, clapping his hands together. "So, son. You've got yourself a girlfriend and a BMW. All you need is two working legs, and the world is your oyster."

"One step at a time," Hugh said. "No pun intended. But we've all got a lot of work to do over the next few months. We're not out of the woods yet."

"All right." I messed with his hair to annoy him. "Let us have five minutes of celebration before you come steamrolling in with your real-life talk."

Hugh held up his hands in surrender. "Fine. In that case, you won't think it's too early for me to point out that it was *me* who said that miracles happen all the time. And you both mocked me, and yet see us now."

Cameron and I both nodded solemnly.

"Yes," Cameron said. "You are now the King of the Optimists."

"Better than the King of the Assholes," I said.

Hugh guffawed while Butch and Cameron looked on, confused.

"I'm not even going to ask," Butch said, and I told him that was for the best.

"Right. We'll let you get some quality father and son time. We both need a good meal and a good night's sleep." We both stood and gathered our things to leave.

"Not too good a sleep, I hope," Cameron said, and then remembered his dad was sitting next to him. "Um, I mean you don't want too much REM sleep, you—"

"We all know what you meant, boy," Butch said good-naturedly as Cameron's cheeks reddened. "See you kids soon."

We walked out of Cameron's room hand-in-hand. Life was going to be good; I knew it. I couldn't bring myself to be overjoyed that the storm had happened since it had caused so much damage, but I did have to wonder whether the three of us would have got together without it. Those hours in the bungalow were truly magical, and I would never forget them.

As we reached the waiting room, we spotted Chrissy again, this time with Vic by her side in a wheelchair. A nurse was wheeling him out, and their faces were all grim.

Since Chrissy managed to style out the destruction of her wedding venue with a smile on her face, something must have been terribly wrong. We decided not to disturb them, but I couldn't help but wave a goodbye at Chrissy, and she gestured for us to come over.

"What's wrong?" I asked, and Chrissy held my hand tight.

"It's Jasmine."

"Has she been in contact with you?" Vic asked, and the urgency in his voice made my blood run cold.

"No. Not since... since she came to see us while we were trapped at the bungalow yesterday morning. Why? What happened?"

Vic shook his head and rose to his feet.

"Ah, sir, please don't—" The nurse realized it was pointless trying to stop him as he approached me and placed a hand on my shoulder.

"She's missing, Muriel. She was supposed to visit her parents last night, but she didn't show up, and nobody's seen her. It's been turned over for us to investigate. I'm so sorry."

My vision blurred. Vic talked about needing answers to some questions about 'known associates' and anyone who might have a problem with her being in town, but I didn't listen properly. I couldn't focus and even less respond. Hugh's strong hands held me in place, but my mind had gone in a million directions at once.

"We have to find her," I blurted out finally.

Right now, nothing else mattered.

The story continues in The Ranch, book two of the Fashionable Friends Trilogy.

ABOUT THE AUTHOR

Stephanie Brother writes scintillating stories with bad boys and step-siblings as their main romantic focus. She's always been curious about the forbidden, and this is her way of exploring such complex relationships that threaten to keep her couples apart. As she writes her way to her dream job, Ms. Brother hopes that her readers will enjoy the full emotional and romantic experience as much as she's enjoyed writing them.

www.ingramcontent.com/pod-product-compliance
Ingram Content Group UK Ltd.
Pitfield, Milton Keynes, MK11 3LW, UK
UKHW040006200726
13854UKWH00001B/68

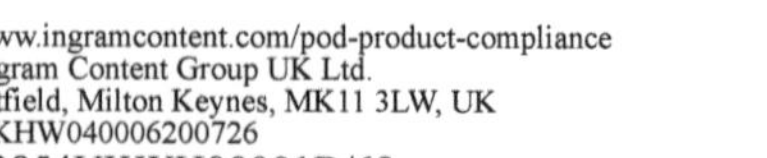

9 798201 144586